MAIGRET
and the
FORTUNETELLER

MAIGRET
and the
FORTUNETELLER

Georges Simenon

Translated by
Geoffrey Sainsbury

A Helen and Kurt Wolff Book
Harcourt Brace Jovanovich, Publishers
San Diego New York London

HBJ

Library of Congress Cataloging-in-Publication Data

Simenon, Georges, 1903–
Maigret and the fortuneteller.

Translation of: Signé Picpus.
"A Helen and Kurt Wolff book."
I. Title.
PQ2637.I53S5413 1989 843'.912 88-16301
ISBN 0-15-155571-0

Designed by Kaelin Chappell

Printed in the United States of America

First United States edition

A B C D E

1

It was three minutes to five. On the enormous map of Paris that covered a large part of the wall, a small white disk lighted up. Seeing it, a man put down his sandwich and thrust a plug into one of the thousand sockets of the switchboard.

"Hello! . . . Fourteenth? . . . Your car's just left? . . ."

Maigret, who was doing his best to look unconcerned, stood, with the sun shining full on him, mopping his brow.

The man at the switchboard grunted something, removed the plug, and picked up his sandwich. It was for the superintendent's benefit that he murmured: "A *bercy*."

This meant, in their professional jargon, a drunk.

It was August, and Paris smelled of warm asphalt. Through the wide-open windows, the roar of the traffic on the Ile de la Cité penetrated this room that was the brain of the police emergency center. Below, in the courtyard of Police Headquarters, two vans packed with men stood ready and waiting to go.

Another disk lighted up, this time in the Eighteenth Arrondissement. Once again, down went the sandwich, in went the plug.

"Yes? . . . Gérard? . . . How are you? . . . What's going on? . . . Is that all? . . ."

Someone had fallen out of a window – or had thrown himself out. It seemed to be the current choice for suicide –

by the poor and the old especially, and mainly in the Eighteenth.

Maigret knocked out his pipe on the windowsill and refilled it, glancing at the clock. It was two minutes past the hour.

Two minutes past! Had they killed the fortuneteller or hadn't they?

The door opened, and Lucas, short, round, and bustling, appeared, also mopping his brow.

"Well, Chief, nothing yet?"

Like Maigret, he had crossed the street that separated the Police Judiciaire from Police Headquarters to be on the spot if any news came in.

"By the way, that fellow's here again. . . ."

"Mascouvin?"

"Yes, and white as a sheet. He wants to talk to you. He says the only thing now is to kill himself."

Another disk lighted up. Might this be what they were waiting for? . . . No. Not yet. Only a fight at Porte de Saint-Ouen.

A telephone call. The director of the Police Judiciaire asking for the superintendent.

"Hello! Is that you, Maigret? . . . Anything happened? . . . Nothing so far? . . ."

A slight emphasis on the last two words, and the sarcasm wasn't lost on Maigret, who looked savagely at the receiver as he put it down. He was hot and would have given a lot for a tall glass of cold beer. For the first time in his life, he was not far from hoping that a crime had been committed.

For if the fortuneteller had not been killed on the stroke of five, he'd been made a fool of, and it would be weeks, if not months, before his colleagues got tired of teasing him about it.

All because of a few words written backward on a piece of blotting paper!

"Go get Mascouvin."

Certainly nobody could have looked less like a practical joker than this Mascouvin. He had turned up at the Police Judiciaire the evening before, and had insisted on seeing Superintendent Maigret in person. Nobody else would do, and he had waited obstinately, his face twitching from time to time with a nervous tic.

"It's a matter of life or death," he had said.

A thin, dull man with glasses, approaching middle age, who could never have been taken for anything but a somewhat seedy bachelor, which indeed was what he was. He fidgeted the whole time he was telling his story.

"I've worked for fifteen years at Proud and Drouin – you know, the real-estate agent on Boulevard Bonne-Nouvelle. I live alone in a little two-room apartment on Place des Vosges. Number 21 . . . Every evening I go and play bridge at a club on Rue des Pyramides. . . . During the last two months I've had such bad luck. It's swallowed up all my savings. . . . I owe the countess eight hundred francs. . . ."

Maigret listened with only half an ear, thinking that at that moment half of Paris was on vacation, while the rest were sitting under the awnings of café terraces sipping cool drinks.

A countess? Who would she be? . . . The wretched visitor made haste to explain that she had once been rich but had fallen on hard times. With almost no assets except a fine apartment on Rue des Pyramides, she had made use of it to start a bridge club. A handsome woman, according to Mascouvin, and it wasn't hard to guess he was in love with her.

"This afternoon, at four o'clock, Superintendent, I took a thousand francs of my firm's money. . . ."

He couldn't have looked more tragic if he had killed a

whole family. Still fidgeting and twitching, he went on with his confession. When he left his office, he wandered around the streets with the thousand-franc note in his pocket, tormented by remorse. He entered the Café des Sports, at the corner of Place de la République and Boulevard Voltaire, where he was in the habit of dropping in for an apéritif before dinner.

"Nestor, bring me some writing paper, will you?"

He always called the waiter by his Christian name. Yes, he would write to his employers and tell them everything, and at the same time send them back their thousand francs. It would be easier than telling them face to face, and he could explain the whole thing – his run of bad luck for two whole months and the countess's pressing him to pay his debt.

Though he adored the countess, she had a soft spot only for a retired army officer who frequented the club.

Nestor duly returned with pen and ink and a folder that contained a few sheets of paper and a blotter.

Mascouvin opened the folder and sat staring at it, not knowing how to begin. Because he was nearsighted and didn't need his glasses for writing, he had put them down on the blotter, and they lay there, the lenses vertical to the blotter. It was in fact the way he'd put them down that was the cause of everything. With the play of light, one of the lenses acted as a mirror, reflecting – the right way, of course – something that had been blotted. It was the phrase *am going to kill*, and his curiosity was immediately aroused. Who was going to kill whom?

Shifting the glasses, he was gradually able to piece together the whole sentence, in fact the whole note – for it was a note someone had written and signed.

Tomorrow afternoon on the stroke of five I am going to kill the fortuneteller. Picpus.

Five past five. The man at the switchboard had had time to finish his sandwich, which smelled of garlic, for the little white disks all over the map of Paris remained obstinately unlighted. Steps could be heard on the stairs. It was Lucas, with the wretched Mascouvin.

The latter hadn't written to his employers after all. The previous evening, after hearing his story, Maigret had advised him to go to work as usual and put the thousand-franc note back where it belonged, without saying anything about it. It had been thought just as well, however, to keep an eye on him, and Lucas was given the job. About half past nine Mascouvin went to Rue des Pyramides and hung around for a while, without going up to the countess's apartment.

He spent the night in his own apartment on Place des Vosges and was at his office at the usual time next morning. He had lunch in a cheap restaurant on Boulevard Saint-Martin.

It was only at half past four that he suddenly decided he could bear it no longer and, leaving the dingy offices of Proud and Drouin, made once again for the Quai des Orfèvres.

"I couldn't hold out any longer, Superintendent. I couldn't look anybody in the face, least of all my employers. . . . I had the feeling . . ."

"Sit down . . . and keep quiet. . . ."

Eight after five. A triumphant sun blazed down on Paris, which seemed to be crawling with humanity, the men walking around in their shirt sleeves, the women nearly nude under their thin dresses. Meanwhile, the police were watching over four hundred eighty-two fortunetellers and clairvoyants!

"Do you think, Maigret, it's a hoax?" Lucas sighed. He was worried, for his chief risked being made ridiculous.

A disk in the Third lighted up.

"Hello! . . . Right! . . ."

The man on the switchboard sighed too, in sympathy. "Only another *bercy* . . . You'd think it was Saturday!"

Mascouvin couldn't keep still. He kept jumping around in his seat, pulling his fingers, and opening his mouth.

"Excuse me, Superintendent, I really must tell you . . ."

"Don't talk!" snapped Maigret.

Had the man named Picpus decided to kill or not?

A lighted disk. Again in the Eighteenth.

"Hello? . . . Superintendent Maigret? . . . Yes, he's here. Hold on a moment. . . ."

Maigret's heart beat a little faster as he took the receiver.

"Hello . . . Yes . . . Rue Damrémont police station . . . What's that? . . . 67 *bis* Rue Caulaincourt . . . Mademoiselle Jeanne . . . What? A fortuneteller?"

His voice had risen to a roar. His eyes glowed.

"Come on, Lucas. Quick! . . . Yes, bring him along too. . . . You never know."

Looking rather like a sleepwalker, a sad sleepwalker, Joseph Mascouvin followed the two men down dusty stairs to where a police car was waiting in the courtyard.

"67 *bis* Rue Caulaincourt . . . Quickly!"

On the way Maigret looked at the list of fortunetellers and clairvoyants that had been compiled, for discreet surveillance, the evening before. Naturally, Mademoiselle Jeanne's name was not among them.

"Can't you go any faster?"

And that fool of a Mascouvin asked timidly: "Is she dead?"

For a moment Maigret wondered whether he was as naïve as he appeared.

We'll see about that! he said to himself.

"Revolver?" murmured Lucas.

"Knife."

There was no need to look for the numbers. A crowd had collected outside the house, which faced Place Constantin Pecqueur.

"Shall I wait down here?" stammered Mascouvin.

"No. Come up. . . . Come on. Follow us."

Policemen controlling the crowd made a way through it for Maigret and his sergeant.

"Fifth floor. The door on the right."

There was no elevator. The house was well kept, however, and the horrified tenants gathered on the landings looked respectable and prosperous. On the fifth floor, the police superintendent of the Eighteenth held out his hand to Maigret.

"Come in. . . . The body's not yet cold. . . . It was only by luck that we got here so soon, as you'll see."

One entered a little room bathed in sunshine, which poured in through a wide bay window opening onto a balcony that looked southward right across the city. It was a pretty little room, neat and cozy, with pale-colored curtains, Louis XVI chairs, and charming ornaments.

A local doctor turned around to greet them with "There's nothing to be done. . . . The second blow was fatal. . . ."

The room was too small for all the people gathered there. Maigret, after filling his pipe, took off his jacket, revealing the mauve suspenders his wife had bought for him the week before. They were even made of silk, and brought a smile to the local superintendent's face. That smile, in turn, brought a scowl to Maigret's.

"Come on . . . Tell us . . . What happened?"

"I haven't had time to collect much information yet, particularly since the concierge is anything but talkative. You have to drag the words out of her one by one. . . . This Mademoiselle Jeanne – her real name's Marie Picard, and she was born in Bayeux. . . ."

Maigret lifted up the sheet that had been thrown over the body. She had been a good-looking woman. Fortyish. Plump and well preserved. Fair hair whose color might not be altogether natural.

"She wasn't registered as a fortuneteller and she never advertised. Still she seems to have had quite a number of people coming to consult her."

"How many this afternoon?"

"I asked Madame Baffoin – Eugénie Baffoin – but she said she didn't know. She said it was no business of hers and that concierges weren't half as nosy as they were made out to be. . . . A few minutes past five this lady . . ."

A lively little woman, also middle-aged, jumped up from her chair. She was wearing a rather absurd hat.

"I knew Mademoiselle Jeanne quite well," she explained. "From time to time she came and spent a few days with us at Morsang. . . . Do you know Morsang? . . . On the Seine, by the barrage a little above Corbeil . . . I have an inn there, the Pretty Pigeon. . . . And since Isidore had caught some fine tench, and I was coming to Paris, I said to myself . . ."

The tench were there in a basket, packed in grass to keep them fresh.

"You see, I knew she was fond of fish, and I thought it would be a little treat for her. . . ."

"How long have you known her?"

"For the last five years or so . . . Once, she came and stayed with us a whole month. . . ."

"Alone?"

"What sort of a person do you take her for? . . . As I was saying, I just dropped in, between errands. I found the door ajar. Just an inch or two – like this. . . . So I simply called out 'Mademoiselle Jeanne! It's me – Madame Roy!' Then, when there was no answer, I came in, and . . . she was sitting at that little table, leaning forward. I thought she'd fallen asleep. I went over to give her a shake and . . ."

Thus, at about seven minutes past five Mademoiselle Jeanne, the fortuneteller, was already dead, with two knife wounds in her back.

"Has the weapon been found?" asked Maigret, turning to the local superintendent.

"No."

"Was the place ransacked?"

"No. As you see, everything seems to be in perfect order. . . . I doubt if the murderer even went into the bedroom. Look . . ."

He opened a door that led to a bedroom, prettier than the living room. A little boudoir, a feminine nest, with frills and pastel colors.

"And you say that the concierge . . ."

"Knows nothing about it. . . . It was Madame Roy here who called us, from the bar over there. . . . We found her on the doorstep. . . . There's just one thing. . . . Ah! Here's the locksmith I sent for. . . . Come in, will you? . . . Open this door for us. . . ."

Maigret happened to glance at Mascouvin, sitting miserably on the edge of a chair, and the Proud and Drouin clerk whined: "I don't think I can bear it, Superintendent."

"Too bad!"

It would be much worse when the Crime Squad experts came on the scene. Maigret wished he had time first to down a beer.

"As you see," explained the local superintendent, "the apartment consists of this room, the simple dining room over there, the bedroom, a storeroom, and . . ."

He pointed to the door on which the locksmith was already at work.

"I suppose that's the kitchen."

The locksmith found a skeleton key that did the trick. The door swung open.

"Well, and who are you? . . . What are you doing there? . . ."

It was so unexpected as to be almost comic. In a clean and tidy little kitchen, in which there wasn't a single dirty plate or glass, an old man was sitting on the edge of the table, where he appeared to be waiting meekly and patiently.

"Answer! What are you doing there?"

The old man gazed blankly at the men who filed into the room, but he seemed unable to answer. The oddest thing of all was that, on this boiling August day, he was wearing an overcoat, one that had turned green with age. His cheeks were covered with an unkempt beard. His shoulders sagged; his look was evasive.

"How long have you been there?"

He seemed to be making an effort, as though the question was difficult to understand. Finally he took a watch out of his pocket, studied it, and said: "Forty minutes."

"So you were here at five o'clock?"

"I arrived just before."

"Then you must have witnessed the crime."

"What crime?"

He was a bit deaf and kept turning one ear toward the local superintendent.

"What? You don't know that . . . ?"

In the sitting room, the sheet was lifted up to show him the body. He gazed at it in stupefaction.

"Well?"

He didn't answer. He stood as though petrified. Then his hand went up to wipe his eyes. That didn't necessarily mean he was crying, however; Maigret had already noticed that his eyes watered continually.

"What were you doing in that kitchen?"

Again the old man stared blankly at them, as though the words had no meaning for him.

"How did you come to be locked in that kitchen?" he was asked again. "And where's the key?"

There was no sign of it on either side of the door.

"I don't know," sighed the old man, like a child who expects a beating.

"What don't you know?"

"Anything."

"Let's see your papers."

The old man fumbled in his pockets, wiped his eyes again, sniffed, and finally held out a wallet with silver initials. Maigret and the local superintendent exchanged glances.

Was the old man really not very bright, or was he acting the part? If the latter, he was certainly doing it to perfection. Opening the wallet, Maigret extracted an identity card, which he proceeded to read out loud.

"Octave Le Cloaguen, Ship's Surgeon (Retired), age 68, 13 Boulevard des Batignolles, Paris."

"There are too many of us here," he growled suddenly. "Send everyone out."

There were indeed a good dozen people in the room, which had become unbearably stuffy.

Joseph Mascouvin got up docilely.

"Not you! Get back where you were, damn it! And keep still . . ."

"You, too. Sit down, Monsieur Le Cloaguen. Come on, now! What were you doing here?"

The old man trembled. Once again he seemed to hear the words without grasping their sense.

Twice Maigret repeated the question, each time louder, and finally Le Cloaguen stammered: "Oh yes! . . . Excuse me . . . I came here . . ."

"What for?"

"To see her." And he pointed toward the body under the sheet.

"Did you want your fortune told?"

No answer.

"Were you one of her customers? Yes or no?"

"Yes . . . I came . . ."

"And what happened?"

"I was sitting here. . . . Yes, on that gilt chair . . . There was a knock at the door . . . like this. . . ."

He went over to the door. Was he going to run? No. It was only to knock in a special way, three or four staccato raps.

"Then *she* said . . ."

"Yes, go on. What did she say?"

"She said: 'In there. Quick!' And she pushed me into the kitchen."

"Was it she who locked the door?"

"I don't know."

"And then what?"

"Nothing . . . I sat down on the edge of the table. . . . The window was open, and I looked down into the street."

"And after that?"

"Nothing . . . I heard lots of voices. . . . I thought I'd better keep quiet."

He spoke slowly, quietly, and even sadly. Suddenly he asked an unexpected question: "Have you got any tobacco?"

"A cigarette?"

"No. Tobacco."

Maigret held out his pouch. Le Cloaguen took a pinch of tobacco and put it in his mouth with visible satisfaction.

"You needn't tell my wife. . . ."

Meanwhile, Lucas had been searching through the apartment. Maigret knew what he was looking for.

"Well?" he asked.

"Nothing, Chief. The key is neither in here nor in the kitchen. I've sent a man down to look in the street, in case it was thrown out the window."

Maigret turned back to Le Cloaguen.

"So, you say you came here at a few minutes before five to consult the fortuneteller. Two or three minutes before the hour, someone knocked in a particular way, and Mademoiselle Jeanne pushed you into the kitchen. . . . Is that right? . . . You sat there on the table looking out the window. Then you heard voices, but you didn't move. . . . You didn't even look through the keyhole. . . ."

"No. I thought she had company."

"Have you been here before?"

"Every week."

"For how long?"

"Very long."

Was he quite right in the head, or wasn't he?

The whole district was in a turmoil. When the cars from the Public Prosecutor's Office arrived, there was a crowd of at least two hundred outside the house. And all in a blaze of sunshine that lighted up the brightly colored awnings over the café terraces. A café terrace! That was the place to be on a day like this, with a cold beer.

Maigret put on his jacket again when he heard voices on the landing.

"So you're here, Superintendent," the deputy public prosecutor said. "I suppose that means we've got something interesting. . . ."

"Unless I've got hold of a couple of half-wits," growled Maigret to himself.

That brute Mascouvin, who couldn't take his eyes off the superintendent. And the old man, snuffling and chewing his tobacco.

Other cars drew up, this time with reporters.

"Here, Lucas! Take these two fellows away. . . . I'll be back at the Quai in half an hour."

Mascouvin peered around for his hat. Before going, he turned back to say, with the same mournful seriousness he gave to everything: "You see, Superintendent, Picpus did kill the fortuneteller!"

2

Curiously enough, it was the sight of a hand, the man's hand resting on a threadbare trouser leg, that made Maigret feel the tragedy that had occurred. For the first time he saw in his companion something more than a puppet – a picturesque puppet – being moved across the stage.

Earlier, in the apartment on Rue Caulaincourt, he had witnessed the "performance," which was the word he found most suitable to describe the descent of the deputy public prosecutor and his minions on the scene of the crime. In the middle of all the hullabaloo, Octave Le Cloaguen had seemed to him a broken-down old creature with eyes that expressed nothing unless it was stupidity. Maigret had been intrigued by the way those eyes went completely blank at times, as though the old man's spirit had flown off to some other place, and could be brought back only by shouting the same question at him three times over.

Later on, in his office at the Quai des Orfèvres, which was like an oven, since it caught the full blast of the western sun, Maigret, sweating from every pore, had questioned the old man closely for over half an hour, at the end of which he knew just about as much as when he started. Le Cloaguen was quite unruffled by the interrogation. He even gave the impression of being anxious to help the superintendent.

And all the time, while Maigret was mopping first his forehead, then the back of his neck, the old man, still in his overcoat, was apparently quite comfortable. Certainly he hadn't perspired a drop. Maigret was sure of it. He had looked carefully.

Now they were driving in a taxi, with all the windows open. It was eight o'clock in the evening, and a deliciously cool breeze circulated through the streets of Paris. Le Cloaguen sat rigid in his seat, leaning forward slightly, and Maigret's eye, for no particular reason, had come to rest on his right hand, a curiously long hand, with knotty joints and skin so old and withered it seemed to be positively cracking in places. The end of the index finger was missing.

Was it that hand? . . . Maigret's mind wandered into fantasy. . . . What a host of things the human hand could accomplish! And this hand, sixty-eight years old . . .

Suddenly a drop fell on the dry skin. They were driving just then along Rue Auber, with cafés on either side and happy crowds jostling each other on the sidewalks. Maigret raised his eyes. The old man stared, blankly, straight in front of him, as before, but his forehead was covered with beads of sweat.

It was so unexpected that Maigret was disconcerted. Why, after facing with equanimity the ordeal of a police interrogation, should Le Cloaguen suddenly be seized with panic? For there was no doubt about it. That sweat had nothing to do with heat. It was caused by fear. It was the outward sign of that interior collapse against which all efforts are in vain.

Had the old man caught sight of something or somebody? It appeared unlikely. Had he been upset by Maigret's staring at his hand? Was that truncated finger somehow capable of giving him away?

The taxi struggled through the crowds around the Gare Saint-Lazare and started up Rue de Rome. The shadows were already turning blue, and the air grew cooler. Yet the beads of sweat became more and more profuse on the old man's forehead, and his color changed to a leaden pallor. Suddenly Maigret understood: *The man was becoming more and more terrified as he approached his home.*

A few minutes later they were on Boulevard des Batignolles, drawing up in front of a big building of gray stone, with a porte-cochere, an interior courtyard, and an air of spaciousness and affluence. The lodge was well kept, and the concierge neatly dressed in black. The staircase was dark, and the varnished steps were covered by a crimson carpet held down by rods.

Le Cloaguen walked up slowly, breathing with difficulty. He said nothing, but his sweating forehead spoke for him. What was it he was afraid of?

Only one apartment on each floor. Handsome front doors of dark oak with well-polished brasswork. On the fourth floor Maigret rang. For a whole minute – and the minute seemed long – they could hear furtive steps inside; then the door opened, only a few inches, but enough to reveal a woman's face on which curiosity and mistrust were clearly written.

"Madame Le Cloaguen?"

The answer came hurriedly.

"Yes. My maid's out, so I had to answer the door myself."

He felt that she was lying. He guessed that she didn't have a maid.

"If I'm not disturbing you, I'd like to have a few words with you. . . . Superintendent Maigret of the Police Judiciaire."

The woman's eyes darted to her husband. She was fiftyish, a small nervous woman, with mobile features – too mobile – and her eyes seemed exceptionally keen. Her glance at her husband lasted only seconds, but Maigret was conscious of its effect on the old man, from whom the smell of fear seemed to emanate.

That was the only sign. His features expressed nothing. He said nothing, explained nothing. Once again his spirit seemed far away, as he stood meekly on the doormat waiting to be admitted to his own home.

The woman, who had recovered her self-possession, stood aside for Maigret to pass, then crossed the hall and threw open the door of a huge room, whose windows were framed by thick curtains, which kept out all but a pale half-light.

"Sit down. . . . What is it? . . . What has he been up to?"

Another sharp look at her husband, who had not even thought of taking off his hat or coat.

Ten years later, Maigret could still have described every detail of that room, with its three tall windows and green velveteen curtains with yellow tassels, its easy chairs fitted with loose covers, the little gilt table, the huge pockmarked mirror over the black marble mantelpiece, the brass dogs in the fireplace . . .

A faint sound behind the door convinced him that someone was listening, someone he guessed to be feminine. He wasn't wrong. He learned later that it was Gisèle Le Cloaguen, the twenty-eight-year-old daughter.

The apartment must be very large, since it occupied a whole floor of the building. Here and there it suggested wealth, yet over it hung a sort of cloud of poverty. Madame Le Cloaguen was dressed in black silk, with a cameo brooch on her bosom and beautiful rings on her fingers.

"First of all, madame, may I ask you whether you know a certain Mademoiselle Jeanne?"

He was sure she didn't. She seemed to try genuinely to place the name. Obviously she had been expecting quite a different question.

"What does she do?"

"She lives on Rue Caulaincourt."

"No. I don't think I've ever . . ."

"Her profession consists of predicting the future. . . . I must tell you something that might upset you. To put the matter briefly, she was murdered in her home at five o'clock this afternoon. And at the same time your husband was in the apartment, having been locked in the kitchen."

"Octave! What were you doing there?"

She turned toward him and spoke with quiet dignity, but it didn't ring true at all. No. That quiet dignity was affected, as false as the bronze ornaments on the mantelpiece. Maigret was convinced that, as soon as he left, the scene would degenerate into a sordid fight.

Le Cloaguen swallowed painfully before answering humbly.

"I was . . . I was there. . . ."

With assumed disdain, she said: "I didn't know you were interested in having your fortune told."

Then, taking no further notice of him, she turned back to Maigret. Fiddling with her cameo brooch and looking very much a woman of the world, she spoke, with increasing volubility.

"I must take you into my confidence, Superintendent. . . . I know absolutely nothing of this business. But I do know my husband. As he may perhaps have told you, he was for many years in the merchant marine, serving as doctor, first on board liners going to South America, then for some years in the waters off China. . . . Something must have happened to him. I don't know what. But he's never been the same since. . . ."

She didn't seem in the least embarrassed by discussing it in front of him.

"You must have noticed yourself that there is something childish about him. . . . It's been a tragedy for us – for my daughter and me – since it has made things difficult for us socially. . . ."

Maigret understood. He looked around the room, picturing it with all the loose covers removed, the chandelier lighted up, and plates of petits fours on the little gilt table . . . women sitting stiffly with cups of tea in their hands. . . .

Later on, the concierge confirmed the picture he had formed, telling him about the weekly receptions, which were generally referred to by the other tenants as the Monday tea fights.

She also told him that Madame Le Cloaguen indeed had no servant, only a cleaning woman who came in for a couple of hours in the morning. For the Monday tea fights a butler was hired from a catering firm.

"And yet they're rich!" said the concierge, who was more talkative than the one on Rue Caulaincourt. "They're said to have an income of two hundred thousand francs a year. A lawyer comes all the way from Saint-Raphaël to see them every year in December, and he hands over their money. What they do with it passes my understanding. Ask the tradesmen around here what they think. At the butcher's, they never buy anything but odds and ends, and not even much of that. And you see how the poor old man's dressed, summer and winter alike. . . ."

But what connection was there between this apartment and the bright, comfortable little rooms on Rue Caulaincourt? Between this thin, nervous little woman, who was terribly self-possessed, and the plump and pretty Mademoiselle Jeanne, who had been killed in her sunny room a few hours before?

Still, the case was only just opening up, and Maigret did not try to jump to any conclusions. He was content to note facts and take stock of the characters involved.

The strange Mascouvin, in his office at Proud and Drouin, at his home on Place des Vosges, and in the countess's bridge salon on Rue des Pyramides . . .

"He's just like a grown-up child, Superintendent," Madame Le Cloaguen was saying. "I really can't put it in any other words. . . . He spends his days wandering around the streets, only coming home for meals. But I can assure you he's absolutely harmless. . . ."

Harmless. The word struck Maigret, and he turned to look at the old man again. The beads of sweat were gone from his forehead, and he had relapsed into a state of complete apathy.

What had he been so afraid of? And why had he now recovered his composure, or, rather, his vacuity?

More rustling behind the door, and Madame Le Cloaguen called out: "Come in, Gisèle . . . This is my daughter. . . . It is she more than anyone who suffers from her father's condition. You know what I mean. . . . It makes it difficult for her to ask friends to drop in. . . ."

Why was Gisèle so badly dressed? And why did she have that scowl on her face, without which she would have been pretty? Her handshake was like a man's. She greeted Maigret without a smile, without the least softening of her expression, and when she turned toward the old man, her look was pitiless.

It was she who said to him, as though speaking to a servant: "Take your hat off."

"Do you know, Gisèle, your father went this afternoon to a fortuneteller, and there's been a scandal. . . ."

Strange, that word, *scandal,* applied to a crime! Evidently, to these two women, the life and death of Mademoiselle Jeanne was of no account. What mattered was that Le Cloaguen had been drawn into the case, had been questioned at the Quai des Orfèvres. What mattered was that a police inspector was now sitting in their living room.

"I'm extremely sorry if I'm putting you out in any way, but, considering the circumstances, I'd like while I'm here to have a look at Monsieur Le Cloaguen's room."

"Gisèle?"

Madame Le Cloaguen threw a questioning glance at her

daughter, who nodded slightly, meaning, no doubt, that the old man's room was presentable.

Maigret made it an excuse to have a good look at the apartment. Quite a comfortable dining room. Madame Le Cloaguen's bedroom had some old but good pieces of furniture. No sign of a bathroom anywhere, but each of the principal bedrooms had its *cabinet de toilette.* The walls of the latter had not been repapered for years, and the floors were covered with odd scraps of linoleum.

"My husband uses his room as a study too," explained Madame Le Cloaguen. "His life at sea gave him a taste for simplicity. . . . That's what he likes . . . the utmost simplicity. . . ."

Hold on! Here was something very odd. Why on earth should the bolt be on the outside of the door, instead of on the inside? Was the wretched man locked into his room?

On this point too, Maigret's suspicions were confirmed by the concierge.

"Yes, monsieur. You'd hardly believe it! When those ladies have their friends in for tea, they lock the poor man up, for fear he'll suddenly come into the room and spoil the party. And it's even said that if he's ever late for a meal, he gets locked up for a day or two as a punishment. . . ."

A little room, hardly worthy of the name, looking out, not on Boulevard des Batignolles, but on a narrow interior well. The window was covered with transparent paper, obstructing still further the little light that reached it.

A dusty unshaded low-watt bulb hung from the ceiling. There was an iron bedstead and an iron washstand on three legs, a chipped enamel jug beside it on the floor. In a corner stood the piece of furniture that gave the place its only claim to be called a study — a monumental desk of black wood, which had probably been bought cheap at an auction sale, and which was much too big for the room.

Le Cloaguen had come in quietly with them, and stood there like a schoolboy waiting for the inevitable punishment. Soon Maigret would go, and then . . .

The superintendent almost had a feeling of guilt at the idea of leaving him to these two women. He thought of that old hand with the mutilated finger, that old hand which . . .

"It's Spartan, isn't it?" said Madame Le Cloaguen, delighted to have found that word. "He could have a more comfortable room any time he likes, but this is what he prefers. Like his clothes. He insists on wearing that old coat all year round. You could not persuade him to change it for all the gold in the world."

And the kitchen, madame? Is it the old man who insists on its being so squalid, with an unscrubbed table littered with dirty dishes, saucepans not scoured for years, and cupboards practically empty? The only food visible was some wretched-looking vegetables and a dish of ragout that was no doubt waiting to be warmed up for their supper.

Gisèle's room was like her mother's, comfortable and well-furnished, but here too was the same dreariness that hung over the whole apartment and made it difficult to believe that, outside, the whole of Paris was rejoicing in the cool air of a perfect August evening and the tender glow of the lingering sunset.

"Have you lived here long?"

"Ten years, Superintendent. Ever since we left Saint-Raphaël. We thought coming north might do my husband good, but it's turned out just the opposite. He's worse than before. . . ."

A strange idea, bring a man north for his health when he's spent most of his life sailing to South America or in the China seas! As though the noise and bustle of Paris would be good for a weak head!

The old man had remained in his room, like a well-trained

dog. Maigret would have liked to see him again and talk to him alone. To speak of sympathy would perhaps be an exaggeration, but he was intrigued by the man and wanted to get to the bottom of the mystery of his miserable existence.

And obviously that was just what this woman didn't want him to do.

"You see! There's nothing mysterious about us. And if my husband suddenly took it into his head to have his fortune told . . . There's no knowing what goes on in a feeble mind like his. . . . I hope, Superintendent, that you'll soon be able to put your hands on the murderer and that this unfortunate business will have no bad consequences. . . ."

No bad consequences for whom? For her, evidently, and that daughter of hers, who was exactly like her. They formed, so to speak, a single element in the case, for there was no doubt about one thing – they would back each other up through thick and thin.

There was something wrong about this apartment. Several times Maigret had the feeling that something was missing, as though a familiar object had been removed. When he looked around, however, he could find nothing to justify the feeling. All the usual items of furniture seemed to be there. Nevertheless, he was unable to shake off the impression, and it kept nagging him.

"Good evening, Superintendent . . . If there's any further information we can give you . . ."

What would happen once the front door was shut? As he walked down the stairs, Maigret pictured the old man in his room, waiting patiently to be set upon by the two furious, raging women.

And suddenly a light flashed on in his mind. He had it! He knew what was missing. In not one of the rooms he had visited had he seen a photograph, neither on the walls nor on the mantelpieces, not even a snapshot, such as is found in the humblest dwelling, no picture of the beach or the mountains.

The walls had been bare, absolutely bare!

Maigret spent a quarter of an hour with the concierge, then went out into the street, where he was joined by Inspector Janvier.

"Well, Chief, what are my orders?"

"Stay here. I think we'd better find out a little more about these people."

On Place Clichy, he went into a brasserie and called Madame Maigret, to tell her he wouldn't be back for dinner. Then at last he settled down to a glass of beer.

The most puzzling thing was that question of the key for the kitchen door. That Mademoiselle Jeanne should have pushed the old man into the kitchen was conceivable, but why should she lock him in? Though it seemed to be his fate to be locked up.

Could the murderer have done it? Why should he? What would make him think there was someone on the other side of that door?

On one point Maigret realized he had slipped up at Rue Caulaincourt. Had the old man left his hat in the living room? No doubt he had taken it off, and if he had been bundled hurriedly into the kitchen, it might easily have been left behind. In that case, the murderer might have seen it, noted the closed kitchen door, and taken the key.

Maigret took out his little notebook and wrote down the word *hat.* He must ask the others. Of all those present, somebody ought to have noticed whether Le Cloaguen had his hat with him when he came out of the kitchen. But, in the midst of all that activity . . .

Or had the old man locked himself in and thrown the key out the window?

As for the other one, Mascouvin . . . Maigret finished his

second glass of beer and got up with a sigh, hesitating between a bus and a taxi.

The life of the streets around him seemed to become less real as the mystery of Rue Caulaincourt gradually took hold of him. The streetlights went on and the passers-by were reduced to mere blue shadows against a paler blue ground. He decided on a taxi.

"Quai des Orfèvres."

"Right away, Monsieur Maigret!"

It was childish, but it was human: it pleased him that the driver recognized him, and the friendliness of the greeting touched him.

Picpus . . .

To whom could he – or she – have written that note in the Café des Sports on Place de la République? But didn't the whole story sound rather fantastic? Joseph Mascouvin, a model clerk, after years of faithful service steals a thousand-franc note from his employers. He goes into a café, asks for writing paper and pen, puts his glasses down on the blotter, and right away sees the announcement of a forthcoming murder!

"Well, Monsieur Maigret, are you hot on the trail?"

Maigret sighed. He paid off the taxi and walked heavily up the stairs of the Police Judiciaire. François, the receptionist, pounced on him before he could reach his office.

"They're waiting for you, Superintendent."

A glance at the huge padded door of the director's room. Maigret understood.

The green-shaded lamp on the desk was lighted, but the curtains hadn't yet been drawn. The windows were wide open on the darkening landscape of the river, and puffs of cool air came into the room.

The director of the PJ looked up. Standing by him was Lucas, a woebegone Lucas, whose eyes avoided his chief's.

"So you were quite right, Maigret. . . . Picpus was as good as his word, and killed the fortuneteller."

The superintendent frowned, because he couldn't guess what this preamble was leading up to.

"Unfortunately, it will be several days before we can get any more out of the principal witness."

Why should the words give Maigret a little stab? He had only known Le Cloaguen for a few hours. And could he really claim to know him? . . . The director's seriousness and Lucas's embarrassment hinted at some further disaster. Could the old man have . . . ?

"It was my fault," murmured Lucas.

Why couldn't they come out with it and tell him what had happened?

"I questioned him for over an hour. . . ."

A sigh of relief! So it had nothing to do with the old ship's doctor. It was about Mascouvin, whom Lucas had been instructed to question once again.

"I wanted to take him to Rue des Pyramides. . . . It was just an off chance. But I thought that if he was confronted by that countess of his, I might be able to drag something more out of him. . . . He'd been quite calm up to then. . . . I intended to take a taxi, but there was no sign of one on the quay, so we started walking. There were a lot of people around, since the Belle Jardinière had just shut, and all the shoppers and clerks were streaming out. . . ."

"Go on."

"It happened so quickly I couldn't stop him. . . . We were crossing the Pont-Neuf. He made a sudden dash for the parapet, and jumped over. . . ."

Maigret filled his pipe and said nothing.

"Unfortunately, he didn't fall straight into the water, but struck one of the piers."

It was easy to imagine the scene. Hundreds of people rushing to the parapet and craning their necks. More people watching from the quays. A hat floating on the surface of the water, and then a dark lump bobbing up and disappearing again. An onlooker throwing off his jacket and plunging in after him . . .

"Luckily, a tug was passing. . . ."

Again easy to imagine. Everybody shouting at the tug and pointing. The tug going full speed astern. One of the crew armed with a boat hook. An apparently lifeless Mascouvin being finally fished out and laid on the black iron deck.

"He's not dead, but that's about all you can say for him. It was his head that struck the pier. . . . He was taken to the Hôtel-Dieu, and he's in the hands of Chesnard, the chief surgeon. . . ."

Maigret struck a match and drew on his pipe.

"What do you think?" asked the director. "Puts a different light on it, doesn't it?"

"A different light on what?" grunted the superintendent.

As for there being any light, he couldn't see it! It was too early for that. All they knew for certain was that Mademoiselle Jeanne was dead, killed by two knife wounds in the back while she was sitting at her little Louis XVI table. . . . If that meant anything, it meant she had been quite unsuspecting. . . .

Le Cloaguen in the kitchen . . . Mascouvin and his countess . . .

"What have you done with the woman?" asked Maigret, blowing out a cloud of smoke.

"What woman?"

"The one who lives at Morsang and keeps the Pretty Pigeon . . . I can't remember her name."

"She wanted to catch a train . . ."

"By the way, does she know Mascouvin?"

Lucas hung his head.

"I didn't think of asking her. . . . She was in a hurry. Said she had a lot of people to look after . . ."

The director couldn't help smiling when Maigret asked finally: "What happened to her fish?"

As though he'd had his eye on it and would have liked to take it home to Madame Maigret for dinner.

3

Almost every quarter of an hour Maigret, sighing and groaning, made an effort as though to lift the world, but it was only his own great lump of a body that he heaved painfully over from one side to the other under the sheet, to sink once again into a sleep peopled with nightmare figures. Each time, he woke Madame Maigret, and, slow to get to sleep again, she stared at the blind, which bellied out in the breeze for a moment and then hung lifeless.

The night was crystal clear, and sounds carried far. On Boulevard Richard-Lenoir she could even hear – or she thought she could – the little train arriving at Les Halles.

At 21 Place des Vosges a window was open too, but there was no one sleeping in the bed, which the concierge had as usual turned down.

Joseph Mascouvin was lying in the Hôtel-Dieu, with half his face concealed by bandages, while a nurse sat knitting by his bedside.

No one sat by Mademoiselle Jeanne. She lay in a drawer in a huge refrigerator in the Forensic Laboratory.

On Boulevard des Batignolles, not far from the lights of Place Clichy, Inspector Janvier got up now and then from his seat to stroll up and down under the trees. Sometimes he looked at the moon, which hung in the sky between two gables covered with advertisements, sometimes at the dark windows of Number 17.

At first, women had sidled up to him – strangely, all of them very fat – but they had soon figured him out and had made themselves scarce. One after another the bars closed their doors. Well before the first paling of the eastern sky, a sudden chill in the air announced the approach of dawn.

On Rue des Pyramides the countess's last guests didn't leave till five in the morning, after eating some sandwiches.

The presses poured forth their newspapers. The Métro threw open its gates. In the little cafés, the gas was lighted under the percolators, and piles of warm croissants were put out on the bars.

Torrence, his eyes still filled with sleep, walked along Boulevard des Batignolles looking for Janvier, whom he was to relieve.

"Anything happen?"

"Nothing."

Maigret had his breakfast in his shirt sleeves. Life began to flow back into the streets, over which hung a faint morning mist.

The young girl in the red hat, having neatened her two rooms and kitchen not far from Place des Ternes, hurried toward the Métro, stopping for a moment on the way to buy her morning paper.

But instead of going to the travel agency on Boulevard de la Madeleine where she worked, she went on for another four stations, getting out at Châtelet and making her way toward the huge dark Palais de Justice. She was nervous, and her lips moved continuously, as though she was rehearsing what she wanted to say.

Standing at his window, Maigret was carefully scraping out his two pipes.

"A young lady wants to see you. . . . She didn't give her name. . . . She says it's very urgent. . . ."

With that, on this bright Saturday morning, another chapter opened in the mystery. The girl wore a navy-blue suit and a red hat. Normally, she must have shown to the world a happy, smiling, dimpled face, but now she was distraught.

"Where is he, Superintendent? . . . Is he still alive? . . . He's my brother, or, rather, my foster brother. . . ."

She was referring to Mascouvin, whose photograph was on the front page of her newspaper, alongside one of Maigret, the same one the newspapers had printed with each new case for more than fifteen years.

"Hello! . . . Hôtel-Dieu? . . ."

Yes, Mascouvin was still alive. He was unconscious, however, and unable to see anybody. The chief surgeon would be seeing him again in a few minutes.

"Tell me something about him, mademoiselle . . . But first of all, what's your name?"

"Berthe . . . Berthe Janiveau. I'm a stenographer at a travel agency. My father was a carpenter in a village not far from Clermont. . . . My parents were quite old when I was born. In fact, they'd given up hope of having a child of their own and had adopted an orphan, Joseph Mascouvin. . . ."

In the presence of this fresh young girl, Maigret assumed a paternal and benevolent air.

"Say, would you mind coming with me to your brother's place on Place des Vosges?"

He took her in a taxi, and she talked the whole way there without his having to ask any questions. The ground floor of the building formed an arcade, and under it two or three people were talking eagerly to the concierge, who held a newspaper in her hand.

"Such a quiet gentleman," she was saying. "So considerate and polite to everybody! . . ."

On the second floor, a former cabinet minister lived. On the third, the landlord. It was only on the fourth that the atmosphere changed. Here four families were crowded into small apartments on either side of a long corridor, where the sun came in through a skylight.

"Why should he want to kill himself?" said Mademoiselle Berthe. "There has never been anything the least tragic in his life. . . ."

So far, Joseph Mascouvin had been, for Maigret, little more than odd and somewhat disconcerting. But Mademoiselle Berthe talked, and his apartment talked too. It consisted of one room, a *cabinet de toilette,* and a little kitchenette. The room was scrupulously neat, and the books on the shelves were serious, even forbidding. A phonograph looked as if it had been recently bought.

"You see, Superintendent, he never thought himself quite like other people. The village children used to call him The Orphan. . . . At school he was always top of his class. At home he was always ready to help. He was always afraid of being a nuisance, of being in the way. He had the feeling he was only there out of charity. . . . My parents wanted him to go on with his schooling. But then they died. And to everyone's surprise, they left hardly any money. . . . I was too young to go to work, and it was Joseph who looked after me. . . ."

"Why don't you live together?"

She blushed.

"He didn't want that. . . . You see, we weren't really brother and sister. . . ."

"Tell me, mademoiselle, was he a little bit in love with you?"

"I think he may have been. . . . But he never said so. . . . He wouldn't have dreamed of it."

"Did he have any friends? Any girl friends?"

"I never knew of any. . . . Sometimes he took me out on a Sunday."

"Did he ever take you to Morsang?"

She looked puzzled.

"Where is it?"

"On the Seine. Just above Corbeil."

"No. If we went to the country, it was on the Marne, at Joinville. We went there quite often. . . . For some time now, Joseph has had a passion for bridge."

"Has he ever spoken to you about the countess?"

"What countess?"

Maigret looked around the apartment discreetly. He didn't like to carry out a thorough search in the girl's presence. Nothing offered the faintest clue. In a desk were notebooks, in which Mascouvin kept accounts, and they too gave the impression of a man meticulously orderly. There were some books on bridge, one or two of them going into complicated analysis.

Mademoiselle Berthe pointed to a photograph hanging on the wall. It was of her parents. They were sitting in front of their house, and she, a little girl, was squatting at their feet.

"Do you think your foster brother capable of stealing?"

"Joseph? Steal? . . . He's the most scrupulous man in the world. . . ."

She laughed a little nervously.

"Of course, you don't know him. . . . I remember once he was in a dreadful state for a whole week, because he couldn't get his accounts to balance. . . ."

"Well, mademoiselle, you seem to have told me all you can, and the best thing now is for you to go to your work. . . . We'll get in touch with you at once if there's any news."

"You will, won't you, Superintendent? . . . Promise you

won't forget . . . Even if I can't talk to him, I'd like to see with my own eyes that he's alive."

Maigret shut the window, took a last look around the room, locked the door, and slipped the key in his pocket. Downstairs, he had a word with the concierge.

No, Mascouvin received practically no mail, she told him, except now and again an express letter from his sister on a Saturday, fixing a rendezvous for the following day. . . . Lately, yes, he had seemed preoccupied.

"Such a considerate man, Superintendent. . . . If there were any children playing in the courtyard, he never passed without speaking to them, and at the end of the month he always had candy for them."

Maigret walked to Place de la République, where he found the Café des Sports practically empty. Nestor, the waiter, was wiping the imitation-marble tables.

"Monsieur Mascouvin? . . . You can't imagine what a shock it gave me when I picked up my paper this morning. . . . That was where he always sat. Over there . . ."

A slot machine near the bar; at the far end, a billiard table – for Russian billiards – with a few tables on one side. It was at one of those tables that Mascouvin always sat, always at the same time.

"No, I don't think I ever saw him speak to anybody. . . . He drank his apéritif slowly, always the same. He read his newspaper. . . . He always gave me twenty-five centimes for a tip. . . . And seeing him come, you knew the exact time."

"Did he often ask you for writing materials?"

"I think it was the first time."

Unfortunately, Nestor couldn't say whether Mascouvin really had written something or whether he had merely stared at the blotter. Nor could Nestor remember who had had the blotter before him.

"In the afternoon, there are so many. . . ."

Maigret sighed and mopped his brow. A moment later he was trundling along on the rear platform of a bus, dreaming wistfully of beaches and long white-crested waves.

"Another young lady to see you, Maigret . . . You seem to be popular with them today. . . ."

A different type altogether from Mademoiselle Berthe. A plump girl, perhaps eighteen, with a large bosom, red cheeks, and bulging eyes. There was almost a smell of milk about her. You couldn't help feeling she'd just come from milking the cows.

The feeling wasn't altogether unjustified, since she worked in a dairy on Rue Caulaincourt. She was so overpowered by her surroundings that she appeared about to cry.

"It was Monsieur Jules who told me to . . ."

"Excuse me. Who's Monsieur Jules?"

"The man I work for . . . He said I must absolutely come and see you. . . ."

She soon felt more relaxed and watched the superintendent smoking his pipe. He had that indulgent, fatherly look on his face.

"Tell me all about it," he said.

"I don't know his name – I swear I don't. . . . It was his car that caught my eye, a beautiful green sports car. . . ."

"A young man, is it? . . . What's he like?"

She blushed. Her name was Emma, and she'd only arrived in Paris a few months before. In the mornings she carried the milk to the houses on Rue Caulaincourt. In the afternoons she served in the shop.

"I really don't know how old he is. And he may be married."

Married or not, he was obviously her hero.

"He's tall and dark and ever so smartly dressed, and he

always has a pale gray hat. . . . Once, he had field glasses in a leather case."

"And he parked his car near Number 67 *bis*, I suppose."

"How did you know? . . . He'd been coming about once a week, sometimes twice. I noticed he went into Number 67 *bis*, and I supposed it was to see a girl friend."

"Why?"

"He was dressed like that. As though he was going to see a woman. . . . I really can't explain it, but that's how it looked to me."

"Have you ever been close enough to have a good look at him?"

Poor Emma! It was so easy to imagine her hovering around, finding any pretext, however silly, to go out into the street to get near him.

"Did he come yesterday?"

She was almost in tears again. She could only nod her head.

"At what time?"

"I don't know exactly, but it must have been about five o'clock. . . . He didn't stay long. . . . But he couldn't have killed the lady – really he couldn't have!"

Of course not!

Maigret didn't contradict her, but questioned her patiently. Her description of the man was more interesting than she imagined. The very details that appealed to her put him into a category well known to the police.

A flashy creature with a diamond ring. His clothes always looking new. A frequenter of race tracks. A useful point perhaps – she had noticed he had two teeth crowned with gold. Maigret would have to find out whether the description tallied with anyone known to the Morals Squad or the Gambling Squad. Also, whether there was anyone like that in the group that went to the countess's bridge club.

"Thank you, mademoiselle . . . Monsieur Jules was quite right to tell you to come."

"He's innocent, isn't he? . . . I simply couldn't believe that a man like that . . ."

What she hadn't confessed – though it's true it had no bearing on the case – was that, more than once, when the green car was parked on Rue Caulaincourt, she had thrown a flower on his seat when she passed.

"You didn't notice anyone else going into 67 *bis* about that time?"

"Yes. A lady."

"What was she like?"

The description corresponded reasonably well with the landlady of the Pretty Pigeon, but Emma was unable to say for certain whether she had gone into the house before or after the man with the green sports car had left.

While she was speaking, Maigret scribbled down some orders: Keep a lookout for all green sports cars. Keep a lookout particularly at the races for a tall, dark man . . . etc.

"Hello! . . . Hôtel-Dieu? . . ."

Mascouvin was not dead. The surgeon himself was at the other end of the line. He gave the patient about one chance in five of recovering.

If he did pull through, there could be no thought of questioning him for another week at least.

"Hello! . . . Mademoiselle Berthe? . . . Your brother's holding his own. . . . Don't worry. . . . No. There's no question of your seeing him at present. . . . I'll keep you informed. . . ."

Maigret sighed again. For a moment his eyes were vacant, while across his retina stretched a long strip of gleaming sand, beyond it a limitless glassy sea. . . .

This was the most discouraging moment in a case. The characters were beginning to take shape, the stage was more or less set, but the actors' parts seemed as yet quite unrelated.

What was happening on Boulevard des Batignolles? Was the old man imprisoned in his miserable room?

Strangely enough, the answer came at once. It was Inspector Torrence calling.

"Is that you, Chief? . . . I'm telephoning from a little bar on the quay. . . . Our man left home on the stroke of nine. . . . What? . . . Oh, yes. He's got his overcoat on. . . . No. He never looked at me. For that matter, he doesn't seem to look at anything. He just walks slowly along, looking straight in front of him, like a convalescent out walking for the first time. . . . Only, now and then he stops and looks in a shop window. . . . He hesitates before crossing streets, as though he's scared of cars. . . . He never once turned around to see if he was being followed. . . . Now he's standing on the quay watching a fisherman. I can see him from here. . . . What? . . . No. He hasn't spoken to a soul. . . . What? . . . Can you speak a little louder? . . . A newspaper? . . . No. He hasn't bought one. . . . Yes, I'll go on following him. . . . I've been lucky enough to find a really good Vouvray in this little bar."

By a narrow back staircase, Maigret, heavy and serious, climbed up to the laboratories under the roof of the Palais de Justice.

He shook hands with one or two of the experts and looked over their shoulders to see their work.

"Well, fellows?"

Nothing of any interest. The writing on the blotter could equally well be a man's or a woman's. No fingerprints on the blotter, but many on the outside of the folder. These had been checked. None of them belonged to known criminals.

Sprightly Dr. Paul, with the perky little beard, had dropped in too to see how things were going.

"Ah! Here's my friend Maigret. . . . A strong one did that

job. . . . The first blow missed the heart by a few millimeters, but the second went right into the left ventricle. . . . I can give you a tip. Standing where he was to deliver the blow, he almost certainly was spattered with blood. It must have spurted out like a fountain. . . ."

There had certainly been no sign of blood on Le Cloaguen's clothes when he was found in the kitchen. If he'd washed them, they couldn't have had time to dry.

"Tell me, Doctor, could a woman have done it?"

"A reasonably strong one, yes. And, you know, when they're strung up, women sometimes have a sort of nervous strength that's extraordinary."

That didn't simplify anything!

Janvier, after only a few hours' sleep, returned to the Quai des Orfèvres.

"Here! Take this photograph of Mascouvin and show it around in the neighborhood of Rue Caulaincourt. See if anybody knows him. . . ."

It wasn't a very hopeful line, but you had to try everything.

Lucas had gone to visit the countess on Rue des Pyramides. He had to wait a long time, because she was still in bed when he arrived. When she finally appeared, she was in a very elegant, fluffy negligee. Very *grande dame*, the countess! She looked at Lucas through a lorgnette and insisted on calling him Monsieur Policeman.

Mascouvin did indeed owe her a small sum of money. Eight hundred francs? It might be that much, but it was a matter of no importance. . . . Goodness no! . . . She would never dream of pressing him for the money. . . . Poor fellow! She was sorry for him. He was rather a fish out of water at her club. After all, he was only a modest clerk, while all the others were men and women of the world – a retired colonel, the wife of a big chocolate maker, the founder and head of a bank. . . .

There were two huge rooms, furnished quite tastefully. In one of them was a little bar, behind which was a pantry where they made the sandwiches for those who stayed late.

"Ask her," said Maigret when Lucas called, "whether she knows a man who . . ."

He described the man with the green sports car. The countess knew nobody like that.

"Just a minute, Lucas! Ask in the neighborhood. It might be that someone has seen the car. Girls have a sharp eye for a fancy car. . . ."

Buses packed with foreigners threaded their way through the streets of Paris, with a guide bawling out the sights through a megaphone. The thermometer registered ninety-five in the shade. The pools were so crowded that swimming was impossible.

"Go get me a beer, will you?" Maigret asked the PJ receptionist. "No. Make it two . . ."

At noon Lucas returned.

"No trace of the green sports car . . . I made a list of the members of the bridge club. It's a registered club, and there doesn't seem to be anything wrong with it. . . . But it's not half such a smart place as the old girl likes to make out. Looks so at first sight; then you notice it's a bit motheaten. I looked into the accounts, which give the winnings, since she gets a percentage. I was surprised to see how small they were. . . . As for the members – a lonely lot, I'd say. People with no family who don't know what to do with themselves. Or unhappily married and anxious to stay away from home as much as possible . . . No doubt the countess reigns over them like a queen. There really is some style about her, and she doubtless gives them all the feeling they're moving in society. . . ."

"Has Le Cloaguen ever been there?"

"He's not on the list."

"Or his wife or his daughter?"

"Not them either."

"What about Mademoiselle Jeanne?"

"Ah! I was coming to her. . . . When I showed her photograph, I had the impression the countess was uncomfortable. She didn't sound quite natural when she asked: 'Who is she?' "

The waiter from the Brasserie Dauphine, who knew the Police Judiciaire as well as if he worked there, came in and put two glasses of beer down on the desk. Maigret drank one at a single draught. As he lifted the other to his lips, he caught the look on Lucas's face and murmured: "Sorry, old friend, I'm just too thirsty!"

After all, Lucas had had his chance, on his way back from the bridge club.

Noon bells rang. Hundreds of Parisians who had a half-day hurried toward the sea or the country.

"Hello! . . . Get my wife on the line, will you?"

The second glass of beer was almost empty. His two pipes lay on the desk in front of him.

"Hello! Is that you? . . . What? . . . No. It's not to tell you I won't be back to lunch. On the contrary. I'll be there in – let me see – about an hour. . . . What I want you to do is pack my brown suitcase. . . . Yes, the brown one . . . We're going to spend the weekend by the river. . . . What? . . . At Morsang . . . See you soon."

"What shall I do next?" asked Lucas, who knew very well he wasn't going to spend Sunday in the country.

And, pencil in hand, Maigret sketched out the work for all of them.

Rue Caulaincourt: Find out if anyone else noticed the green sports car. Ask all the tradespeople, all the café waiters . . .

Boulevard des Batignolles: Doubt there's much to be gained by following the old man around. Watch his wife for a change.

Place des Vosges: Just as well keep an eye on Mascouvin's house, to see if there are any strange comings and goings.

Anything forgotten? . . . Oh, get the telephone people to register all calls to the Le Cloaguens and to the countess. . . . You never know.

As for the man with the two gold teeth, the Morals Squad and the Gambling Squad would be looking out for him, especially at the races.

"Till Monday, Lucas."

"Have a good time, Chief."

Maigret had put on his hat and was making for the door, when he had another thought.

"Just one thing more – that Mademoiselle Berthe. Perhaps it's silly, but never mind that. I'd like to know on Monday what she's been doing over the weekend."

"Is she pretty?"

"Quite a peach . . . Nice girl too."

And Maigret hurried down the dusty staircase of the PJ.

4

There are days that, without one knowing why, seem to epitomize a season, if not a whole period of one's life, days that seem to play on the whole scale of one's feelings. That Saturday night at Morsang and the Sunday that followed remained for years in Maigret's memory as symbolizing all that was meant by a summer weekend on the river, with its easygoing pleasures and the simple joy of being alive.

The lamps, lighted after dinner under the trees . . . The leaves, the soft deep green found in old tapestries . . . The thin white mist over the steadily moving water of the Seine . . . The laughter at the tables, and the dreamy voices of young people in love . . .

The Maigrets were already in bed when someone brought a phonograph out to the terrace, and for a long time they listened to the tuneful, if not very edifying, music and to the crunch of gravel under the dancers' feet.

Did the superintendent really go to sleep? Their room was in the annex of the Pretty Pigeon. It had an outside iron staircase like a ship's, and a long balcony running right around the second floor. The rooms were as small as cabins, whitewashed, and of cabinlike simplicity, with an iron bed, a washstand, a chair, a few hooks on which to hang clothes, and bright cretonne curtains. That night everybody slept with doors and windows wide open to the August night.

"Do you have enough room?" whispered Madame Maigret, squeezing herself against the wall.

No. He certainly didn't! The bed was much too narrow for two. He dozed off, but it wasn't long before the sound of oars wormed its way into his consciousness. It was about three o'clock. He knew at once what it was – Isidore, the inn's jack-of-all-trades, taking the boat to go and lift his nets.

A little later a baby started crying. Most of the people there were young couples. There were two dentists, an insurance agent, several girls who were saleswomen for chic Paris dressmakers – altogether a friendly, jolly, informal crowd.

"Maigret, where are you?"

Turning over, Madame Maigret saw her husband in the half-light, leaning over the balcony, his suspenders hanging in loops over his haunches, a thin blue streak of smoke going up from his pipe.

"You'll be wanting to sleep all afternoon! . . ."

Wisps of thoughts straggled idly through his mind: Mademoiselle Jeanne came often to the Pretty Pigeon; she danced too. . . . The other visitors were unaware of her profession. . . . She was friendly with the regulars, and in particular used to go out boating with Madame Rialand, the wife of one of the dentists. . . .

A train passed, on the other side of the Seine. A boat came noiselessly toward the little dock. It was Isidore returning. He was a tall, thin, angular man with a drooping mustache, wearing leather waders that came right up his thighs. . . . He walked off toward the kitchen carrying a pail full of live roach and gudgeon.

People began to wake up. A man dressed for fishing came out of one of the ground-floor rooms and, filling his pipe, went over to get his tackle from a shed.

Another emerged, and the two shook hands. . . . Isidore reappeared. He took something, a long object wrapped in paper, from a locker in his boat and stowed it away out of sight in another boat, which was newly painted a pale green.

Everything that was done seemed to have a certain ritual quality, as if it had been done on every fine Sunday morning, for the same eager fishermen embarking at break of day.

Isidore wiped the dew off the thwarts of the green boat, then fetched some rods and lines and laid them out carefully.

Presently a pleasant smell of coffee drifted over from the kitchen, where one of the servants was already at work, her hair unbrushed, no underwear under her apron.

A Monsieur Blaise occupied the room next to the Maigrets. He came out on the balcony, nodded, and went down the iron stairs. He was one of the most regular customers, according to Madame Roy. A quiet man, middle-aged, punctilious about his personal appearance, and, for that matter, about everything else.

In the kitchen, a basket was already waiting for him, with half a chicken, a half-bottle of Burgundy, cheese, fruit, and a bottle of mineral water. Isidore walked down with him to his boat, the green one, which had a little outboard motor.

Little by little it grew lighter, and other fishermen, who had come no doubt from the village on the other side, could be seen under the trees along the riverbank. The motor was started. Alone in the stern, Monsieur Blaise sat with his hand on the tiller, smoking a cigarette, steering his boat upstream, a pike line ending in a spinner trailing in the wake.

"Did you sleep well . . . ?"

"And you . . . ?"

More people emerged from their rooms, some in dressing gowns, some only in pajamas. The day was getting into its stride. The two maids, now neatly dressed, ran to and fro carrying breakfast trays to the rooms.

"Are you out there, Maigret? . . . What are you doing?"

Nothing. Merely letting his thoughts wander . . . Mademoiselle Jeanne . . . Curious that Madame Roy should arrive on the scene with her basket of fish within a few minutes of the murder. . . . Far more curious still, their finding an old man locked in the kitchen, and no sign of the key . . . Was Le Cloaguen merely pretending to know nothing of what had happened?

The children were having breakfast at little tables under the trees. Scantily clad couples carried highly varnished canoes down to the water. A young man with thick glasses hoisted the sail of a tiny dinghy painted royal blue.

"Aren't you going to fish?" asked Madame Maigret.

No. He wasn't going to do anything. It was after nine o'clock when he made up his mind to shave and dress. He breakfasted on cold sausage and a glass of white wine. As far as the eye could see, the Seine was dotted with rowboats, canoes, and little white sails, and every fifty yards along each bank was a fisherman standing still as a statue.

The hours flowed by as smoothly as the river itself. Soon the tables were being laid for lunch. Two or three carloads of people from Paris arrived to join the guests. Madame Maigret, who could never sit idle, had brought some embroidery. On principle, because they were spending a day in the country, she sat on the grass, though she would have been more comfortable in one of the many deck chairs.

The boats began to return; some of the fishermen too. Though the enthusiasts, like Monsieur Blaise, had taken their lunch with them.

Blaise must have gone around the bend into the next reach, toward Seine-Port, for there was no sign of his boat all afternoon. Though, it was true, the other bank, a little upstream, was so overgrown with rushes as to look like a sort of aquatic jungle. They formed a convenient retreat for lovers, and his boat too might well be hidden by them.

Isidore was always busy. He drew off the wine, drove the

car to Corbeil to fetch the meat, and caulked the seams of a leaky boat.

At three o'clock Maigret was dozing in a deck chair. Madame Maigret kept a protective eye on him, almost ready to tell the people around them to keep quiet.

He was, however, only on the borderline of sleep, sufficiently conscious to hear the telephone ring. He looked at his watch, got up, and reached the house just as one of the maids ran out to say: "Monsieur Maigret, you're wanted on the phone."

It was Lucas, who had been given Boulevard des Batignolles and told to call at three.

"Is that you, Chief?"

Ah! There was a slightly penitent tone in the sergeant's voice.

"Something terrible's happened, though I assure you I took every possible precaution. . . . Several times during the morning I noticed that one of the curtains moved, but nobody could possibly have known what I was, because I was dressed up as a tramp. . . ."

"Idiot!"

"What? . . . What did you say?"

Everybody in the Police Judiciaire knew that Maigret hated anything in the nature of a disguise. But there was no stopping Lucas, who loved nothing better than to act a part.

"Well, Chief, at eleven o'clock . . ."

"Who came out?"

"The woman. She didn't so much as glance around, but walked off toward Place Clichy, where she took the Métro. . . . I followed, but . . ."

"She gave you the slip!"

"How did you know? . . . She got out at Saint-Jacques. You can imagine what it was like on a Sunday. Not a soul around . . . except for one solitary taxi. She made straight for it, got in, and drove off. I rushed around trying to find another. . . . No luck . . ."

"Of course not . . ."

"I took the number of hers. . . . Well, Chief, it was fake. There was no such number registered. . . . After changing my clothes, I went back to Boulevard des Batignolles."

"So you're Lucas again!"

"Yes . . . The concierge told me Madame Le Cloaguen hadn't yet got back. The old man's probably locked up, since he hasn't gone out. Nor the daughter either."

On that hot Sunday the streets of Paris would be more than usually empty. And the distant Boulevard Saint-Jacques had no doubt been chosen as being the least likely place for a wandering taxi. . . .

Maigret's face had become serious.

"All right," he grunted.

"What shall I do next?"

"Watch the house, and call me when she gets back . . . By the way, have a good look at her shoes. See if they're dirty . . ."

"I understand, Chief."

Which wasn't true at all. Lucas had no idea what Maigret was thinking. It was no more than the vaguest hunch.

The superintendent came out of the telephone booth and wandered around the inn. He smiled at Madame Roy, who smiled at him, though her smile was rather sad.

"When I think of that poor woman, Superintendent . . ."

"Do you know if she had any particular friend among her clients?"

"No. I don't know that she had. She kept to herself. . . . Her table was over there. Every time I catch sight of it, tears come to my eyes. . . . She adored children. That was probably why she was friendly with the dentist's wife, Madame Rialand, who has two, Monique and Jean-Claude. . . ."

Maigret stood on the threshold. He no longer looked as if he was enjoying a beautiful Sunday. One detail worried him: that solitary taxi standing at the Saint-Jacques station. No question of its being an accident. It had been waiting for her. And it meant that the people involved in this affair were well-organized professionals.

Had that nervous little Madame Le Cloaguen disappeared for good? Somehow the superintendent couldn't bring himself to believe it. Then why should she have found it necessary to escape from police observation for a few hours? To meet someone? To take something – a document, for instance – to where it would be out of their reach? To . . .

A distant but persistent throbbing caught Maigret's ears. He recognized it at once as the sound of the little motor on Monsieur Blaise's boat. Looking up, he saw it approaching, the bow lifted right out of the water, and a minute or two later he watched the fisherman, lounging in the stern, turn his boat in a wide circle, bring it alongside the dock, and cut the motor.

Two or three people who'd been strolling about, Maigret among them, went down to the dock as he arrived. Isidore too went down, to tie up the boat.

"Any luck, Monsieur Blaise?"

And he, not one to make a fuss, casually answered: "A couple of pike . . . Not too bad . . ."

He opened the locker. In a cloth were two pike with grass around them to keep them fresh.

Blaise caught Maigret's eye and, as he had in the morning, gave him a reserved nod, as one does in a country inn.

He stepped out of the boat and strolled toward his room. Maigret hadn't failed to notice his shoes, which were devoid of any trace of dirt.

Isidore took charge of his fishing tackle. He looked up at Maigret when the latter, with the air of an ignorant townsman, asked: "Did he catch them with a spinner?"

"I don't think so. . . . I gave him some live bait, and he probably used that. . . . The chief thing is to know where to go. Monsieur Blaise knows the good fishing spots, and it isn't often he comes back empty-handed."

"Do you mind if I have a look?"

Maigret stepped down into the boat, almost overturning it. He stooped and picked up one of the pike.

"Not bad at all!"

"Middling! . . . Six or seven pounds . . ."

But a sharp look had come into Isidore's eyes, and he took the fish from the superintendent's hand.

"Excuse me. I must get them wrapped up. He'll certainly want to take them back to Paris. . . ."

And Isidore went off to the kitchen.

"What are you doing, Maigret?" asked his wife placidly.

Nothing. He wasn't doing anything. He was just waiting for something. . . . He pretended to be interested in a little sailboat that was trying to move upstream, though there was hardly a breath of wind.

There! He had it! A sudden spurt of joy in the middle of his chest! . . . A flash of triumph in his eyes! . . . After all, you couldn't help getting a kick out of a thing like that. . . . And Maigret had known it was coming. . . . Yet it was not just intuition, based on shaky details. It was a good deal of luck.

The luck, for instance, of a narrow bed for two on a hot night, which had driven him out to the balcony of the annex before the break of day, to witness Isidore's actions.

He hadn't been watching for anything in particular, but as an idle onlooker he had noticed everything. He had seen the man take something long and white from the locker of his own boat and stow it away in the one Monsieur Blaise was going to use. Isidore had spoken of live bait, but the long parcel certainly wasn't that. The live bait was in a can that had holes pierced in the lid. . . .

Though Maigret had noticed everything, he had thought nothing of it. Why should he?

It was Lucas's telephone call. . . . From that moment Maigret's mind had been groping. . . .

Then those two pike . . . Maigret had had a good look at them. He had done a little fishing in his day. If he'd never been an expert, he at least knew the technique.

One thing he knew was that a pike is the most voracious of all fresh-water fish, and nothing is harder than to take the hook out of its mouth. Sometimes you had to cut right down to the stomach.

Blaise's pike, however, hadn't a wound – not even a scratch. . . . They hadn't been caught on a line at all, but in one of Isidore's nets!

When Maigret had picked up the pike, Isidore had given him a sharp look, and the superintendent wasn't in the least surprised now to see the man come from the kitchen and slink around behind the inn to the annex, where he went up the iron stairs and slipped furtively into Blaise's room.

To let Blaise know!

Dear Madame Maigret! With wifely solicitude she said quietly: "You ought to have brought a book. . . . You don't seem to know what to do with yourself."

Yes. Isidore was certainly eyeing him as he came down the iron stairs, moving rather like a cat or a poacher.

"Why don't you sit down?"

Blaise's window was open, and he could be seen changing into his Paris clothes.

"Tell me, Madame Roy . . ."

"Yes, Superintendent?"

A few question asked in a casual tone of voice . . .

Yes, Monsieur Blaise came by train on Saturday evenings, and caught the six o'clock train back on Sundays. He would have to be off soon to catch the ferry above the dam.

No, he never came by car.

Women? What a funny idea! He didn't seem to bother with them. No, he certainly never came to the Pretty Pigeon with one.

What? In one of the houses on the other bank? . . . She had never thought of such a thing! An absurd idea, since he spent his whole day fishing. . . . And anyhow, the few villas on the other side were occupied by most respectable Paris families. There were the Mallets, who had a big river-transport business. Their office was on the Quai Voltaire. . . . Then there were the Durroys, an elderly couple who . . .

"Hush! Here he comes!"

Though he must have been about Maigret's age, Blaise looked considerably younger. He was obviously a man who took good care of himself and saw to it that nothing interfered with the smooth tenor of his life.

"Well. Madame Roy . . ."

"I hear you've had a good day's fishing, Monsieur Blaise."

"Pretty fair . . ."

In a slightly teasing tone she went on: "And a good nap too? Getting up as early as you do, a little sleep when your boat's in the reeds?"

"I never sleep in the daytime," he answered coldly.

"No offense meant, I assure you. Only just now Monsieur Maigret was saying to me . . ."

A keen look from Blaise. A little too keen, too spontaneous. Could he not know who the superintendent was?

The telephone rang again. Maigret was not surprised to hear Lucas's voice once more.

"She's back, Chief. Not in a taxi. She walked from the direction of Rue d'Amsterdam."

"What about her shoes?"

"Dirty . . . As soon as she'd gone in, the old man came out. He seemed quite calm, and started his walk as usual. . . . I have an inspector watching while I call you. . . . What do I do next?"

That was Lucas's usual question. Maigret gave him minute instructions.

"Well," he said, returning to Madame Roy, "so Monsieur Blaise has gone . . ."

He looked into the distance, where the ferry was just crossing the stream, but he didn't see the man.

"How is it he's not crossing, Madame Roy?"

"Just as you were called to the telephone, there were some other people leaving by car."

"People he knew?"

"No, I don't think so. . . . In fact, I'm sure he didn't, by the way he spoke to them. He asked them if they'd mind giving him a lift as far as Corbeil, because he was afraid of missing his train."

"Did he take his fish with him?"

"Oh, yes. He had the package under his arm."

"Whose car was it? Do you know the number?"

She looked bewildered. "I don't know. They'd only dropped in for something to drink. Whatever are you thinking of, Superintendent? A man like Monsieur Blaise! . . . I always ask his advice when I have a little money to invest. He knows everything about stocks and bonds. . . ."

"Do you know his address in Paris?"

"I couldn't tell you offhand. You'll find him in the telephone book. . . . But really, I can't imagine what makes you think . . ."

"I don't think anything, Madame Roy. . . . Here we are . . . B . . . Bardamont . . . Berger . . . Blaise, H., 25 Rue Notre-Dame-de-Lorette . . ."

Madame Roy smiled uneasily. "Only I don't understand. . . . I can't see why you . . . But, of course, they always say the police suspect everybody on principle!"

"May I use your telephone again?"

Corbeil. The stationmaster. No, the Paris train hadn't yet come in. Due in two or three minutes . . . Description? . . . Right . . . Call you back.

Paris. Police Judiciaire.

"25 Rue Notre-Dame-de-Lorette . . . Who's on duty? . . . Dupré? . . . All right. But tell him to try to look natural . . ."

Madame Roy went back to her kitchen. She was annoyed.

"Give me a small calvados."

Maigret sipped it while he waited for the call from Corbeil. When it came, he was not surprised to learn that nobody answering to Monsieur Blaise's description had boarded the Paris train.

Two hours later, the roads were thick with cars returning to the city. At the Pretty Pigeon, the remaining guests were just sitting down to dinner when the telephone rang again. This time it was Dupré, to say that Blaise had not yet returned home.

"Are we spending another night here?" asked Madame Maigret. "I'm thinking about that narrow bed. . . . Not that I mind for myself. It's you I'm bothered about. You got hardly any sleep last night. . . ."

Never mind about that. They'd stay. Later on, when Isidore went down to see that the boats were properly tied up, Maigret was standing by the water's edge with an inscrutable look on his face.

"They're a funny lot, aren't they?" he said suddenly.

"Who are?"

"Fishermen. Can't bear to come back empty-handed. It's their pride. . . . They rely on you to . . ."

At first Isidore was taken aback. Then he grinned and gave Maigret a wink.

"For one of our best customers," he said, "we couldn't very well . . ."

The phonograph was brought out again, but this time there were only three couples to dance under the big trees.

Eleven o'clock. Telephone. Dupré at last.

"Monsieur Blaise has just shown up. . . . What? . . . Pike, did you say? . . . No, I didn't see any pike. . . . No, he wasn't carrying anything. . . . You want me to stay, Chief? . . . Right. I understand."

Hundreds of Parisians were returning, the smell of the country still in their nostrils, their cars full of wild flowers gathered in the woods.

"Hello, Chief!"

Lucas again.

"Nothing . . . The old man got home at seven o'clock. Since then nobody's left. . . . I guess they're all in bed now. There's no sign of a light. . . . I'm turning over to Janvier. . . . Good night, Chief."

It was rather like the curfew of olden days: "Citizens, sleep in peace."

The final call was from the man on duty on Rue Caulaincourt.

"Nothing to report . . ."

Nevertheless, on that beautiful Sunday, something had happened, though it was too soon to say what. All that had been visible so far was like those little bubbles bursting on the surface of the water, which reveal the presence of a fish pushing its nose into the weeds on the bottom.

"Suppose we ask for another room? Then you can have a bed all to yourself. . . ."

The moon rose. The phonograph stopped, and the gravel crunched under the feet of the last couple as they made their way inside.

5

That afternoon Maigret was not far from being ashamed of his profession. From time to time, like an actor whose face suddenly relaxes as he steps off the stage, he slipped into the next room to join Lucas, who was feeling much the same as his chief.

"Still nothing?" the sergeant's eyes asked.

Still nothing. The superintendent gulped down a mouthful of beer and went over to the window, where he stood, cross, anxious, a look of disgust on his face.

"What's *she* doing?" he asked.

"She's getting more and more worked up. She's given up asking for you. Says she wants to see the director."

It was a good thing Madame Le Cloaguen was here; she provided the one bit of comic relief. It was Octave Le Cloaguen who had been summoned to the Quai des Orfèvres, two hours ago, but when the taxi arrived, it was the thin, wiry woman who had jumped out, leaving her husband behind.

Maigret had watched the scene from his window, had smiled, and given instructions to one of his men.

She had given her name to the receptionist. "Le Cloaguen."

"Do you have an appointment? Are you Octave Le Cloaguen?"

"I want to see the superintendent. I can explain it all to him."

That was funny enough. But while she, arguing all the way, was taken to the waiting room – aptly named – another man went down to get her husband, patiently sitting in the taxi.

"Did my wife say I was to go up?"

"The superintendent wants you."

"Where's my wife?"

Three hours had gone by since then, during which the old man in the faded overcoat had been sitting in the same chair, facing the window, in Maigret's office.

Each time the latter returned, after a few moments of relaxation in Lucas's room, he found Le Cloaguen's light-blue eyes turned on him with the same look, the look of a dog who knows it has nothing much to expect from humans, but also that there's no escape from their domination.

There was no mistaking it: that was the meaning of his look. And it was painful to see, for one couldn't help realizing the years of hopeless suffering that had produced it.

Two or three times he had asked: "Where's Madame Le Cloaguen?"

"She's waiting for you."

That didn't reassure him. He knew her quick temper and domineering character, and couldn't possibly imagine her waiting patiently.

Maigret had started his interrogation in the classic manner, *à la chansonnette*, speaking in a friendly, casual tone, as though he attached little importance to the questions he was asking, as though he considered them merely a matter of form.

"There's a small point I want to get cleared up. I forgot to ask you the other day. . . . When there was that special knock on the door, Mademoiselle Jeanne was reading the cards for you . . . ?"

Le Cloaguen listened carefully but with no sign of comprehension, and he made no answer.

"Mademoiselle Jeanne pushed you into the kitchen and shut

the door. . . . Now what I want to know is whether she gathered up the cards or whether they were still on the table. . . . Take your time. Think about it carefully . . . The examining magistrate attaches – God knows why! – an importance to that question that I consider exaggerated."

Le Cloaguen didn't move. He sighed. Once again his hands were resting on his knees, those remarkable hands that had attracted Maigret's attention in the taxi.

"Come on! Try to picture the scene. . . . It was hot. The window was open onto the balcony. . . . The many-colored cards were lying on the marble Louis XVI table. . . ."

The old man's eyes seemed to be saying: "Can't you understand what you're doing to me? You're torturing a poor creature who can't stand up for himself. . . ."

Maigret, ashamed, turned his eyes away, and murmured: "Answer me, please. . . . This is not an official interrogation. Your answers are not being written down. . . . Were the cards lying on the table?"

"Yes."

"You're sure?"

"Yes."

Maigret went over and opened the door. There was a frown on his face and an irritable ring in his voice as he called to Lucas: "Look here, Sergeant! . . . What was that you told me about Mademoiselle Jeanne's never using cards? Monsieur Le Cloaguen tells me a different story, and I see no reason to think he's lying. . . ."

A nasty trick no doubt. As a former minister of the Interior said, the police are not choirboys. Don't their adversaries use every dirty trick devised by man?

"It's quite right," answered Lucas. "We've checked up on that. There wasn't a card in the place. Mademoiselle Jeanne used a crystal ball."

"Well, Monsieur Le Cloaguen? What am I to make of

that? . . . But perhaps you didn't quite understand my question. Think again. Were there really cards on the table?"

Beads of sweat stood out on the old man's forehead.

"I . . . I don't know . . ." He faltered.

"That's all, Lucas. . . . Forgive me if I touch on a rather delicate matter, Monsieur Le Cloaguen. But I'm not blind, and I couldn't help noticing that your family life is not exactly happy. . . . That being the case, you have perhaps, like many men your age, tried to find consolation elsewhere. You looked for a little feminine sympathy, a little human warmth. . . . Am I right? . . . From the very beginning, I found it difficult to believe you're the sort of man to have your fortune told. . . . And if you were hustled like that into the kitchen, wasn't it because you hadn't gone to Rue Caulaincourt as one of Mademoiselle Jeanne's clients?"

The old man didn't dare say yes. He didn't dare say no. All he could do was wonder what new blow the superintendent was about to deliver each time he reappeared from the next room and when he paused to light his pipe with exasperating slowness.

"You're the only person who can help us. We know precious little about that poor woman. Merely that she came to Paris from somewhere or other and worked for a dressmaker, first sewing, then as a model. Later she had her own dressmaking place on Rue Saint-Georges, called Chez Jeanne. That name stuck to her. . . . The dressmaking business wasn't a success, and she went to live on Rue Caulaincourt. . . . And that's all. . . . What about her family? Who were her friends? . . . That's what we want to discover."

"I don't know anything."

"Come on, now . . . I can quite understand your discretion. But don't forget that our only aim is to punish your friend's murderer. . . ."

It was terrible. Suddenly the old man began to weep. Hot

tears ran down his cheeks. He didn't make a sound. He didn't make the slightest movement – not even to wipe them away – but sat just as before, with his long knotty hands still on his knees. Maigret had to turn his head away. To hide his own feelings, he went to the window and stared at a string of barges being towed down the river.

"Of course this is no business of your wife's, and you can count on me not to repeat anything to her. . . . Since you're well off, I take it that you helped Mademoiselle Jeanne financially. . . . Certainly someone helped her. Her clientele wasn't large enough to keep her going – not in the way she lived. Although there was nothing luxurious about her life, she seems to have been comfortable. . . . You have an income of two hundred thousand a year, haven't you?"

No answer. Maigret looked over some papers on his desk.

"One of my men made some inquiries about you, and what we've found out is very much to your credit. It seems that thirty years ago you were the doctor on board a ship going to the Far East. One of the passengers was a rich Argentine breeder, traveling with his daughter. . . ."

Maigret pretended to consult documents on his desk.

"Yellow fever broke out on board, and it seems to have been due entirely to you that panic was averted. And you saved the life of the young girl into the bargain. . . . Then you came down with the disease yourself, and were put ashore at the next port. . . . Among the passengers you were quite a hero, and the rich Argentine, in gratitude for what you had done, settled on you an income of two hundred thousand francs a year for the rest of your life. . . . I can only congratulate you, Monsieur Le Cloaguen. . . . Returning to France, you married the young lady you were engaged to. You left the sea and gave up the practice of medicine. You settled down in Saint-Raphaël to lead the pleasant life of a man of private means. . . . Unfortunately, as she grew older, your wife became more and more penny-pinching, more and more domineering. Since you came to Paris the situation has changed for the worse. . . ."

The old man seemed only to be wondering how long the ordeal would last. Again and again it seemed to be over. Maigret would get up from his chair and make for the door, smiling, like a man whose job was finished, then change his mind and ask one more question – one last point that needed clearing up.

"By the way . . . that finger of yours . . . I understand you had a little accident. At Saint-Raphaël, wasn't it, just before you left? You were chopping wood. I suppose you liked to do it for the exercise, since you had two servants. . . . You missed your aim and cut off the top joint of your index finger. Of the right hand, unfortunately. You must find it rather a handicap.

"Well! I'm finished."

The old man seemed by now to understand Maigret's technique, for he made no move to get up. But his eyes seemed to ask: "Is it really over?"

Not yet!

"Yesterday, someone was talking to me about you. I think I've got his photograph somewhere. . . . Here we are! . . ."

It was a snapshot of Monsieur Blaise, taken without his knowledge as he walked along the street.

"I've forgotten his name. . . . What is it? . . . He seemed to know you quite well. . . ."

It didn't work. Le Cloaguen looked at it blankly. If his face expressed anything at all, it was relief, as though he had been afraid of something else.

"You don't remember him? . . . Oh, well, never mind. . . . He said it was some years since he'd seen you. . . ."

Maigret went into the next room, where Lucas greeted him with a wink.

"If you keep him much longer there'll be sparks flying in the waiting room. His wife's beside herself. She's going to write to the papers! She demands to see the director! In fact, she's going to make real trouble."

Well, she'd been waiting more than three hours. Yet that was nothing to the poor man's ordeal with Maigret. Maigret wasn't going to be deterred, however. The man had him guessing. There was some mystery there, and he couldn't rest till he had unearthed it. It was exasperating. . . . At the same time, he couldn't help feeling a strange sympathy for the wretched man, a sympathy that wasn't merely pity.

So the *chansonnette* continued.

"Dear, dear, we don't seem to be getting anywhere, Monsieur Le Cloaguen. The examining magistrate has just called me to say more evidence has come to light, which makes things more complicated than ever.

"A man who lives across from 67 *bis* Rue Caulaincourt has come forward to say that just after five o'clock last Friday he saw a man throw something out of one of Mademoiselle Jeanne's windows. We wondered what happened to that key. . . . It's been found. . . ."

"I don't care," sighed Le Cloaguen.

"Yet it makes your position worse, doesn't it?"

Maigret laid a key on the desk.

"But you know very well it's not true, Superintendent," murmured the old man with a gentleness and simplicity that were disarming.

"Look, Monsieur Le Cloaguen! . . . Why can't you be frank? Can't you see that you're putting yourself in a very awkward situation? . . . There you are, a wealthy retired doctor who has had a career of distinguished service to be proud of. . . . And the next thing we see is a wretched creature who wanders aimlessly along the streets and who is treated by his own family as a person of no account and locked up to keep him out of the way. . . . What happened to produce such a change? . . . Why did you leave Saint-Raphaël and come to Paris? . . . Why . . . ?"

Le Cloaguen raised his head. His pale-blue eyes had a tragic candor in them as he said very quietly: "You know why. . . . I'm mad."

"What you mean, I think, is that other people – your wife and daughter perhaps – have tried to persuade you that you're mad."

He shook his head. Firmly, though without the least vehemence, he repeated: "No. I'm mad."

"Try to realize the seriousness of what you're saying. If you *are* mad – and I don't believe it for a moment – there would be no reason why you shouldn't have killed Mademoiselle Jeanne. . . . For we never know what a madman may be capable of . . . You suddenly get the idea while you're sitting in her apartment, and for no reason at all you kill her. . . . Then, recovering your senses, you realize the enormity of what you've done. To escape the consequences, you hide in the kitchen, locking yourself in and throwing the key out the window. . . ."

No answer.

"Was that what happened?"

Maigret was almost afraid the old man would say yes, though it would bring the case to an end and save a lot of trouble. But the response was quite otherwise. It had taken him the best part of four hours to get an answer that really sounded as though it meant something.

"I'm mad, but I didn't kill Jeanne."

"You see! You call her Jeanne. So you admit there was some sort of intimacy between you. . . . Why not tell me all about it? . . . You needn't be ashamed. We're used to hearing confessions. . . ."

"I've nothing to say. . . . I'm tired . . . very tired. . . ."

Simply, humbly he added: "And thirsty."

Once again Maigret went into the next room. When he reappeared he was holding a large glass of beer. The old man took a long draught, his Adam's apple going up and down, up and down.

"Where did your wife go on Sunday between eleven and four?"

"I didn't know she went anywhere."

"Were you locked in your room?"

No answer. Le Cloaguen hung his head. What wouldn't Maigret have given for one moment's real frankness! Innumerable men, of all sorts and conditions, had sat in that chair at the Quai des Orfèvres, to be subjected to the same unremitting interrogation, yet none of them had been so completely baffling. It was intriguing, and it was irritating. For an instant, anger almost got the better of him, and he felt like . . .

"Look, Le Cloaguen, you really can't pretend you know nothing at all – not even why you're locked up in your room like a mangy dog. . . ."

"It's because I'm mad."

"A madman wouldn't admit it."

"Yet I'm mad, all the same. . . . Really, Superintendent, I've done nothing wrong. I didn't kill her, and you're making a mistake in . . ."

"Then, damn it, tell me about it!"

"What do you want me to say?"

Either he was the stupidest man on earth or else . . .

"Look me in the face . . . Here on my desk I have a warrant for your arrest. If your answers aren't satisfactory, I can have you locked up here and now."

The situation became even more baffling. For instead of being frightened, the old man seemed reassured. The prospect of going to prison seemed to please him.

Perhaps anything was preferable to the tyranny of those two women.

"As man to man, tell me, why don't you put up a fight? Why don't you stand up for yourself? All your neighbors talk about you, some with pity, some with contempt. . . ."

"My wife looks after me."

"By letting you wear the same coat summer and winter – a coat a tramp would be ashamed of? . . . By not giving you enough money to buy tobacco? . . . Yesterday, you were seen picking up a cigarette butt in the street, like a pauper – you, a retired doctor with an income of two hundred thousand francs a year!"

No answer. Maigret got angrier.

"You're locked up in a filthy little room that was probably never meant for anything but a storeroom. You're kept hidden from their friends as though you're a leper! . . ."

"I assure you they look after me."

"You mean they don't let you actually die of starvation! . . . And you know very well why, Monsieur Le Cloaguen. The money that rich Argentine settled on you was settled on you for life. For life! Do you understand that? You talk as if it was kind of them to keep you alive!"

Was it possible that the old man was a saint?

"I assure you, Superintendent . . ."

"I think you'd better go before I lose my temper. . . . Listen! I'm not going to arrest you yet. I'm going to give you a little time to think things over. And the sooner you make up your mind to tell the truth, the better it will be for you. . . . Lucas! Lucas!"

Lucas came in and noted Maigret's red face. His chief looked really angry.

"Bring in Madame Le Cloaguen."

And once again the old man's hands began to tremble and

his forehead was covered with beads of sweat. Was it possible that those two women actually beat him?

"Come in, madame . . . And may I ask you to leave the talking to me? . . . Silence! . . . I know you're upset with the hours of waiting, but you've only yourself to blame. . . . Don't interrupt me, please! . . . It was your husband who was summoned here, not you, and it seems to me he's old enough to come by himself. Another time, you won't be allowed into the building. . . . But since you brought him here, you can take him away again. I don't know whether we'll want him again, but he'll probably have to be examined by doctors to establish whether he's sane or not. . . . You can go now. . . . Did you hear me? I said you could go. And if you have any complaints, make them to anybody you want. . . . Good-bye, madame . . ."

When the door was shut, Maigret heaved a deep sigh. Lucas was quite concerned to see his chief in such a state, but the latter's features soon relaxed, and he looked at the sergeant with a rueful smile.

"Well?"

"Nothing, Lucas . . . absolutely nothing . . . I don't see that woman in the picture, that's all. . . . I only wish we had found *her* in the kitchen on Rue Caulaincourt. . . ."

Lucas smiled. Never had he seen Maigret so angry.

Now, suddenly, the superintendent became pensive. His thoughts seemed to hang in suspense as he gazed out at the luminous haze over the Seine and the seething multicolored mass of humanity swarming over the Pont Saint-Michel.

"What are you thinking?"

"Nothing . . . We must find out where that woman was on Friday afternoon, exactly where. . . . You see to that."

"Why don't you ask her what she was up to on Sunday?"

"Because!" Because he was convinced she was expecting it and had her answer ready. In fact he had a shrewd suspicion that her anger was due, more than anything else, to her not having been given the opportunity to use it. At that moment, as she drove home in a taxi, she was no doubt prey to nameless terrors.

"Do you think . . ."

"I don't think anything at all. . . . Who knows? . . . Perhaps I'll go to Saint-Raphaël. . . . As for that other phenomenon, our idiotic Mascouvin . . . have you checked the Hôtel-Dieu?"

"His condition's satisfactory. His sister went to see him, but he didn't know her. It'll be a few more days. . . ."

"And the man with the green sports car?"

"Nothing. We've checked up on twenty green sports cars and drawn a blank each time. He's probably changed cars by now."

There was a knock on the door. It was the receptionist.

"The director wants you, Superintendent."

Maigret and Lucas exchanged glances. It was never good, in the middle of a case, to be sent for by the director. It meant he wanted you to explain things you couldn't, or someone was trying to get in your way, complaints were being made, God knows what.

Maigret wasn't in the mood to accept any advice, still less a reprimand. The very way he stuck his pipe in his mouth was sufficient warning.

He went through the padded door.

"You sent for me?"

In silence, the director, perhaps displeased, perhaps amused, handed Maigret an express letter just delivered.

Monsieur Director of the Police Judiciaire,

I have the honor to bring certain facts to your notice and to request an explanation of them. If the latter is not forthcoming, I shall feel obliged to lodge a formal complaint elsewhere.

On Sunday last, returning from my usual weekend at Morsang-sur-Seine, I learned that an individual who said he was an inspector from the Police Judiciaire had shortly before had an interview with my concierge, whom he had questioned at length concerning me, my financial resources, and my daily habits.

My concierge failed to ask this individual for any proof of his identity, and from what she told me I believe him to have been an undesirable person masquerading as a policeman.

I looked out of my window and immediately noticed a man in a little café called the Old Pouilly on Place Saint-Georges. This man was obviously keeping my house under observation.

I live alone and take my meals in a restaurant, and I could only suppose he was waiting for my departure to break into my apartment.

I make no secret of the fact that I speculate on the stock market, as any honest French citizen has a right to. I keep a considerable sum of money at home, as well as a number of bonds, and these would provide a very lucrative haul.

I immediately called the local police and explained the matter, asking for protection. Soon after, a uniformed policeman arrived in Rue Notre-Dame-de-Lorette.

To my great surprise, I saw the man who had been watching the house greet the newcomer. The two men shook hands, and a moment later the one in uniform shrugged his shoulders and went away.

The next morning, the watcher was still there. He was joined by a middle-aged person, coarse-featured and badly dressed, with a pipe stuck in his mouth, who went with him for a glass in the Old Pouilly.

Seeing Maigret's scowl, the director suppressed his smile. It was obvious that the superintendent was not amused.

I could not help thinking that an organized gang was after my money. Throughout the whole of Monday I was followed by a succession of individuals of various shapes and sizes who had, however, one thing in common — they were unprepossessing.

Finally, when I paid my usual weekly visit to Proud and Drouin, who take care of my investments, I discovered that the pipe-smoking gentleman had already been there to inquire whether I was one of their clients.

I would be grateful, Monsieur Director, if you would give your immediate attention to this matter and put an end to a state of affairs that gives me much anxiety.

In the hope you will lose no time in dealing with the matter,

I have the honor to be,

Your obedient servant,

Emile Blaise

"Well, Maigret?"

The look on the superintendent's face had not changed as he read the letter. He had not been amused at the references to himself.

"What do you think of it?"

"I think Monsieur Blaise is laughing at you."

"And at you too, perhaps?"

"At me too."

"Is it true you went to Proud and Drouin?"

"It is. . . . And I had extremely good reason. . . . It's too long to tell you in detail now. . . . You remember Mascouvin, who brought us the famous blotter. . . . Well, he works for Proud and Drouin."

"What's he got to do with Blaise?"

"Wait! Who discovered the crime? A certain Madame Roy, who owns the Pretty Pigeon at Morsang . . ."

"I still don't see . . ."

"Mademoiselle Jeanne went frequently to Morsang. Monsieur Blaise goes there almost every week. And he goes to catch fish that have already been caught. . . ."

"Tell me, Maigret, should I begin to see . . ."

"I'm beginning to think it makes sense. Mascouvin informs us of a crime before it is committed. . . . Mademoiselle Jeanne is killed at the given time. . . . Madame Roy discovers the body a few minutes later. . . . Monsieur Blaise is a client of Proud and Drouin and a client of Madame Roy. . . . But Le Cloaguen . . ."

Maigret mused for a moment.

"Two points of contact already: Proud and Drouin, and Morsang. . . . I think I'll go this evening and take a bridge lesson. . . ."

"A bridge lesson?"

"At the countess's . . . She seems to be a very distinguished woman. She's come down in the world, however, and has to scrape along by running a bridge club for lonely people in her rooms on Rue des Pyramides. . . . I wonder if Blaise ever goes there."

"Suppose he does?"

"It wouldn't prove anything, I know. But it would be a curious coincidence, another link with Mascouvin. So far they only connect via Proud and Drouin. . . . If only Le Cloaguen . . ."

The director shrugged his shoulders, which meant: Well, this is not the time for me to be contrary.

He held out his hand.

"Good luck, old fellow! . . . As for Blaise, perhaps you'd better use a certain discretion. He seems to be rather touchy and only too ready to make trouble. . . . Sounds as though he has a deputy up his sleeve. . . ."

Certainly, certainly, Monsieur Director, Maigret said to himself, but you have not just spent nearly four hours with the haunting Le Cloaguen.

6

The name Picpus had by now become famous. Not only had innumerable experts looked through their microscopes at the upstrokes and downstrokes of his blotted words, but millions searched daily for his name in the headlines of their morning papers. The name had become a standing joke.

"You haven't seen Picpus?"

"Well, how's Picpus today?"

And taxi drivers, ever resourceful, added a new epithet, for their careless fellow drivers: "What do you think you're doing, Picpus?"

It was a fly, a common house fly, that betrayed his identity. Maigret had got up later than usual that morning, because he hadn't left the countess's until two in the morning. The air had not lost its morning coolness, however, though the sun was already gilding the houses in a way that promised another stifling day.

Maigret always loved wandering through the streets while Paris made its morning ablutions and, instead of going straight from Boulevard Richard-Lenoir to the Quai des Orfèvres, he made a detour through Place de la République.

He had cut an absurd figure the evening before on Rue des Pyramides. The moment he arrived, the countess had rushed up to him in a swirl of floating gauze, which gave her the appearance of a *grande coquette* of the Théâtre-Français.

"Hush! Don't say a word! Come this way, my dear Superintendent . . . If you only knew what a flutter I'm in to receive such a celebrated person in my home. . . ."

She led him into her boudoir. She talked. She went on talking. She begged Maigret not to make a scandal in her salon. . . . The members of the club were such well-educated people, such well-connected people. . . .

"Only just now I was saying to the prince . . ."

Her hands were loaded with rings encrusted with imitation jewels. One hand stayed on the superintendent's knee as she looked appealingly into his face, while he stared back.

"Would you really like to spend the evening with us? . . . No, I don't know a Monsieur Blaise. . . . Sometimes a member brings a friend along. . . . No, I can't remember anybody like that. . . . We're really quite a small circle. . . . The whole thing's entirely friendly, though of course everyone contributes something toward the expenses in these difficult times. . . ."

Five minutes later she was introducing Maigret as a retired colonel, regardless of the fact that his photograph appeared regularly in the papers. Then she sat him down at her own table, the one for beginners, to give him a lesson.

Between hands she found time to visit all the other tables, to say in a dramatic stage whisper: "You know who he is, of course. . . . He's the famous Superintendent Maigret. Only he's here incognito, to get my advice about something."

Now, as he wandered along the street, he told himself that Paris was full of strange people, mysterious or amazing, who never came to light until something happened.

He reached the Café des Sports on Place de la République and went in. Hesitating between the bar and the lounge, he finally chose the latter, and as he looked for a table it suddenly occurred to him to sit in Joseph Mascouvin's favorite place. As he did so, his mind automatically reverted to the strange note, to Picpus. Why Picpus? It was the name of a busy street and a small cemetery.

"Waiter! A glass of beer, please."

"Right away, Superintendent."

With his sleeves rolled up, Nestor had been cleaning the bar. There was only one other customer, a girl with a suitcase, presumably from the country, who sat over a cup of coffee, waiting for someone.

"How's that poor Monsieur Mascouvin getting along, Superintendent?"

Nestor bent over to put the beer down on the table. Maigret looked at his bald head, or, rather, he watched a fly that had lighted on it.

The fly crawled for a moment across the bald head, then flew off, to settle next on a calendar. Maigret's eye wandered with it, and suddenly a queer noise came from his throat and he almost jumped up from his seat. The astonished waiter looked around to see what could have startled a police inspector famous all over France for his placidity. He saw nothing.

But Maigret had discovered Picpus!

Yes, there was Picpus. On the wall right in front of Joseph Mascouvin's usual seat. He must have been staring right at it when he studied the writing on the blotter.

What a laugh the public would have if a picture of Picpus appeared in the papers!

Directly over the slot machine hung an enormous calendar, whose real purpose, while telling you the date, was to advertise a firm of furniture movers.

When you move, call . . .

In bright colors, a sort of vulgar Hercules was depicted. He wore a striped jersey inflated like a balloon by his enormous muscles. He had a bright red face, and he winked roguishly at the public as he casually lifted a wardrobe with one hand.

When you move, call . . .

Beneath the beefy wardrobe-juggler, in large letters, was:

PICPUS

And in smaller type:

PICPUS MOVING COMPANY
101 *Rue Picpus, Paris*

So Picpus had never existed. At least, not as a murderer. He was no more than the figment of an advertiser's brain.

Someone had sat in that café writing a letter. When it came to the signature, he – or she – had hesitated. What name should he use? His eye had wandered, had lighted on the advertisement.

Perhaps with a sly smile on his lips, he had signed *Picpus*.

So far, so good! But who had sat there writing in violet ink with the scratchy pen that the Café des Sports provided for its customers?

Only one thing was certain: He hadn't made a mistake. He knew!

"Waiter, what do I owe you?"

Maigret would have liked to take the calendar, for his crime museum, but not now. He'd come back and ask for it when the inquiry was finished.

Since he was only a few steps from Boulevard Bonne-Nouvelle, why not take the opportunity to call on Proud and Drouin? When he'd gone there before, he hadn't been able to see the owners.

The building was full of offices. The stairway was gloomy.

Maigret went straight up. He had already seen the name of the firm on all the windows of the third floor.

"Monsieur Proud, please."

"Do you wish to see him on a personal matter?"

"Personal, yes."

"Monsieur Proud has been dead three years," said the receptionist with a self-satisfied smile.

Maigret, annoyed, asked for Monsieur Drouin.

A few minutes later he was ushered into the office of Monsieur Drouin, a mistrustful-looking man in his fifties.

"Sit down, Superintendent. I would be only too glad to be of assistance to you, though I confess I really can't see . . ."

"I understand, Monsieur Drouin. But I'm afraid it's necessary for me to ask you a few questions."

"If it's about one of my clients, I must warn you that we maintain absolute secrecy about their affairs. In fact, we consider ourselves as much bound by professional secrecy as any doctor. . . ."

"Will you tell me, Monsieur Drouin, if you consider Joseph Mascouvin an honest employee?"

"If I didn't, I would have got rid of him long ago."

"Does he have an important position here?"

Drouin got up and opened a door to make sure no one was listening.

"Under the circumstances, and in view of the mystery surrounding this unhappy young man, I may as well tell you frankly that I've kept him on more out of charity . . ."

"You're not satisfied with him?"

"Try to understand. I've no complaint whatever to make about him. On the contrary. He's always the first to arrive and he's never in a hurry to leave. He's the last person in the world to have a newspaper or a novel tucked away, or to sneak off to smoke a cigarette. He never asks for a day off on the grounds of someone in the family being ill, or the death of a grandmother. . . . The trouble with him is he's too conscientious."

"What do you mean?"

"I suppose it does sound absurd. . . . I've no doubt it has something to do with his having been an orphan. He's oversensitive. Always afraid of not doing enough. Always making mountains out of molehills. . . . He doesn't fit in with the others. And I can't blame them. He's touchy and hardly says much."

"You're quite sure he's never helped himself to any money?"

"Helped himself to money? . . . Really, Superintendent, that's quite impossible. Not only for him, but for anybody else. For the simple reason that there's no money to steal, that is, short of forging a check on the firm's account. This isn't a shop with a cash register, you know! We sell houses, farms, châteaux, building sites, and the money involved runs into hundreds of thousands, if not millions. We never see any cash in this establishment."

"You mean to say your employee couldn't possibly have stolen a thousand francs from you?"

"It is out of the question. . . . As I told you, the man's character . . . No, Superintendent, you're on the wrong track altogether."

"And you keep no money here at all?"

"Only the petty cash. I was forgetting that. But he wouldn't have access to it, and in any case there wouldn't be anything like a thousand francs in it. Besides, if he'd taken twenty, it would have been noticed almost at once and reported to me. . . . No, I'm afraid . . ."

He rose to his feet to indicate he had other work to do.

"Just one more question, which I think you can answer without any breach of professional etiquette . . . Is Monsieur Blaise a big client of yours?"

Drouin hesitated. But he was anxious to get rid of his visitor, and somewhat reluctantly he answered:

"Not in a big way, no. . . . Not that he isn't a man of substance. When he first came to us, his bank references were excellent. But when it comes to actual buying, no. He's really no more than a dabbler. And, strictly between ourselves, more trouble than he's worth. He takes up a lot of our time, but has bought only two or three properties in the course of the last five years. . . . And now, if you'll excuse me . . ."

He didn't offer his hand, and it was with visible satisfaction that he shut the door behind Maigret.

The latter went down the stairs more puzzled than ever. Why should Mascouvin have accused himself of stealing a thousand francs from his employer?

There was a worried, anxious look on Maigret's face when he reached his office, to learn that the examining magistrate had been waiting for him for the last hour. There was another one who was no doubt getting impatient and thought it was high time to get some results.

His pipe in his mouth, Maigret went the back way into the Palais de Justice and made his way to the corridor where the examining magistrates' offices were, and where men under criminal indictment stood guarded by policemen, and witnesses paced up and down, looking at their watches, wondering how much longer they would have to wait. The atmosphere was like that in a steam room.

"Come in, Superintendent. Sit down. . . . I've studied the report you handed in last night and talked it over with my deputy. We're both of the same opinion. Either your Octave Le Cloaguen . . ."

Why did he say "your"?

"Well, either he is really mad – which I'm now beginning to doubt – or he knows a lot more than he'll admit. . . . To settle the matter, I've ordered a medical examination for this afternoon. He'll be seen by two psychiatrists in the presence of our Dr. Paul. What do you think?"

He was pleased with himself, It was almost as though he was throwing out a challenge to the superintendent. He seemed to be saying: "Of course I know you have your methods. But they strike me as being too slow, my poor Maigret. They're old-fashioned. . . . And you might remember that an examining magistrate isn't necessarily a fool and from his office he can unravel problems the police don't understand."

Maigret smoked in silence, and nobody could have guessed what was going on in his mind.

"I've also sent a writ to Saint-Raphaël for evidence to be taken on everything relating to the Le Cloaguen family and the way they lived. . . ."

The examining magistrate was beginning to be disconcerted by Maigret's silence. Was he offended? Might he throw his hand in, refusing to have any more to do with the case?

"You'll excuse me, I'm sure, if I'm forcing the pace. You'll admit that in a case of this sort, which has been given wide coverage, the public is apt to get impatient if they think nothing is being done."

"You're quite right, Magistrate. Only, I wonder . . ."

"What?"

"Nothing. . . . I may be mistaken. . . ."

To tell the truth, Maigret was uneasy. He pictured the old man in his office the day before, with his strange hands resting on his knees and tears streaming down his face. Above all, that pathetic look in his eyes, which seemed to beg his fellow creatures not to take advantage of his defenselessness.

It was odd that the examining magistrate should have said "your Octave Le Cloaguen." . . . The fact was, he had hit the nail on the head!

"When does the examination take place?"

"At three o'clock. Let me see . . . It's eleven now. . . . The family was notified about half an hour ago, by messenger."

"Where's it to be?"

"At the apartment on Boulevard des Batignolles. . . . Though, of course, if the doctors think it necessary, they can take him away and keep him under observation. . . . Will you be there?"

"Possibly."

"Then, my dear Superintendent, I may be seeing you later. . . ."

Admittedly, Maigret was somewhat vexed at their having gone ahead without consulting him first, though it couldn't be denied he'd given them an excuse by arriving so late at the Quai des Orfèvres.

But it wasn't really that that made him sulky and cross. It was something different. Hard to explain . . . *His* Octave Le Cloaguen . . . Well, yes! . . . He had the feeling that he was the only one capable of delving into the old man's mind. Right from the start, in the apartment on Rue Caulaincourt, he had been intrigued by him, and from that moment the old ship's doctor had never left him in peace. It was about him he had been thinking as he gazed at the Herculean Picpus with the vulgar wink. It was about him he was thinking in Monsieur Drouin's office, though ostensibly he was preoccupied by Mascouvin and Blaise.

"Come in, Lucas."

Lucas was obviously aware of the steps that had been decided on in his chief's absence, and he studied the latter out of the corner of his eye.

"Who have we got on Boulevard des Batignolles this morning?"

"Janvier."

As Maigret stood staring out the wide-open window, a verse he had had to learn by heart in school suddenly came back to him:

The seas are so tranquil,
So pure are the skies,
But the sailor's widow
Has tears in her eyes.

Wasn't his fate much the same? The Seine flowed by, a veritable river of peace, and, watching the people in the streets, you would think the whole population was basking in the August sunshine and abandoning all care for the simple joy of being alive. Elsewhere, that same summer sun was shining down on fishermen, on swimmers, as here a symphony of car horns filling streets and boulevards mounted to the blue skies.

So pure are the skies . . .

Yes, his was a strange job! A couple of knife wounds in the back of a woman he had never seen or heard of . . . An old man sweating from fear . . . A clerk who throws himself into the Seine from the Pont-Neuf . . . A blatant advertisement on a calendar in the Café des Sports . . .

"What are we going to do, Chief?"

"Monsieur Blaise?"

"At this time of the morning he'll be on his way to the Bourse. He goes there every day. . . . Ruel's keeping an eye on him."

Not a sign of the green sports car or the dark man with two gold-crowned teeth. Emma, the dairymaid, spent half her time staring out into the street, hoping to see the beautiful car and handsome driver, half dreading what might come of it if she did. A dozen photographs had been shown to her, but she hadn't recognized him in any.

"Get me that travel agency near the Madeleine."

Still with the worried look on his face, Maigret took the receiver from Lucas.

"Hello! . . . Mademoiselle Berthe? . . . Yes, Maigret . . . No. On the contrary. He's getting along nicely, and it won't be long before he's himself again. . . . What time do you leave your office? . . . At noon? . . . Would it bore you to have lunch with me in a little restaurant nearby? . . . What? . . . Good. I'll come right away."

He took a taxi and drew up on Boulevard de la Madeleine just as all the shops and offices were casting out their floods of employees. It wasn't long before he spotted the little red hat and the smiling dimpled face, which nevertheless had a slightly anxious look.

"I can assure you, mademoiselle, that I have no bad news for you. I merely wanted to have a little talk."

People turned around to look at them, thinking no doubt that this middle-aged man had done pretty well for himself.

"Do you like hors-d'oeuvres?"

"Love them."

He chose a little restaurant where he knew there was an abundant choice and secured a table by the window. When the waiter brought a bottle of Alsatian wine, its long thin neck protruding from an ice bucket, it did indeed look as if the middle-aged gentleman was stepping out!

"Tell me, Mademoiselle Berthe . . . when your parents died and your brother provided for your education . . . Take some of those mushrooms. . . . I was saying: When your parents died, I suppose he sent you to a boarding school?"

"To a convent school at Montmorency."

"It must have cost him quite a lot, didn't it?"

"I couldn't bear to think of it. I knew he didn't earn much. But he always said he owed everything to my parents, that it was the least he could do. . . . I'm sure he had to deny himself a great deal to take care of me."

"How long did you stay there?"

"Till I was eighteen. After that, I wanted to live with him, as I told you. It would have been so much cheaper for him. But he wouldn't listen to me. He got the little apartment I have now, near Place des Ternes."

"Furnished?"

"No. He said furnished apartments were generally in rather dubious houses. Not the right thing for a girl my age."

"That was about five years ago," muttered Maigret pensively.

"Exactly. You've worked it out right. I'm twenty-three now."

"Look here, mademoiselle, when we've finished our lunch would you think it a nuisance to show your place to an old man like me?"

"Not at all . . . Only . . . what shall I say to the concierge?"

"That I'm a friend of your brother's. . . . And now let's put our minds on lunch. With my ridiculous questions, I've ruined your appetite."

Other men, middle-aged like him, were eating around them, also with young and pretty girls.

"Yes. I insist that you have dessert."

He got a taxi.

The girl looked at her watch. "We'll have to be quick. I must be back in the office at two."

A quiet street, contrasting with the noise and bustle of Place des Ternes.

"It's here. There is an elevator."

On the fifth floor, three rooms that were admittedly tiny, but there was a brightness and gaiety that suited Mademoiselle Berthe.

"You see, it's quite plain. . . ."

Maigret expected to find suites of furniture, such as are displayed in the windows of the big stores. He was mistaken.

Every piece had been carefully chosen. Not luxurious, of course, but definitely good quality . . . What might it all have cost Mascouvin? . . . Twenty thousand? Perhaps twenty-five.

"Would you like to see the kitchen? I make my own meals, of course. I have hot water at the sink. . . . For the trash . . ."

Proudly she opened a sort of panel, revealing a chute.

"It's a quarter to two. . . . I may have to wait for the bus."

"I'll take you back in a taxi."

"Drop me somewhere near. . . . I don't want the others to think . . ."

Mascouvin . . . Le Cloaguen . . . Mascouvin . . . Le Cloaguen . . . Maigret's mind wandered incessantly from one to the other of these two. . . . Even when he tried to think about the man with the pike. . . . Monsieur Blaise was continually fading into the background. Perhaps because the superintendent couldn't work up any great interest in him as a human being.

"Many thanks for the lovely lunch, Superintendent . . . You're really sure that Joseph's all right?"

On the terraces of the cafés, people sat digesting their too-copious meals. Others, off to the races, forced their way onto already full buses.

With the medical examination at three, it wasn't worth while going back to the Quai des Orfèvres. To fill in the time, Maigret sauntered up Boulevard Malesherbes and Rue de Miromesnil. Even so, it was only half past two when he reached Boulevard des Batignolles. He looked up and down the street for Janvier.

The inspector hailed him from a little restaurant for chauffeurs and taxi drivers, where he had just finished eating and was sitting over a calvados.

"A calva for you, Chief? . . . It's not bad at all. . . .

Nothing much has happened this morning. The old man came out as usual about half past eight, and I followed him around, after asking the local police to keep an eye on the apartment building. . . . He doesn't go fast, the old man, but he covers the ground all right. We went all the way to the Bois de Boulogne, coming back via Porte Maillot. He got home at a few minutes to twelve, without having spoken to a soul. . . ."

"Did the local man report anything?"

"I asked him. . . . Neither of the women left the house. Some meat and vegetables were delivered. No doubt they ordered by phone . . . At half past ten a bicycle messenger from the Palais de Justice . . ."

"I know."

"Oh! Then you know everything. . . . I was late getting lunch, because the place was packed with people from a factory. While I was waiting for a seat to be free, I strolled over to Place Clichy to telephone headquarters. . . . What do you think of this calvados? . . . Honest-to-God stuff, isn't it? . . . It's in little places like this that . . ."

A car stopped in front of the building opposite. Maigret stood up.

"Pay the check, will you? . . . I'll be seeing you soon."

"Shall I stay here?"

"Yes."

A second car drew up. Two gray-haired men got out, and a hefty fellow who was no doubt a hospital attendant. He carried a large bag.

They were joined by the examining magistrate and Dr. Paul, from the first car. As the superintendent approached, the latter greeted him.

"Hello, Maigret! . . . I didn't know you were coming. . . . What do you think of the man? Is he mad or isn't he? You must have an idea. . . . Good afternoon, professor. Hello,

Delvigne . . . Amnesia perhaps? . . . Unless he's pretending . . ."

Maigret was introduced to the two psychiatrists. It was all very cordial and good-natured. Nobody could have guessed that these courtly elderly gentlemen had come to decide whether one of their fellow creatures was to be left to enjoy his freedom or put under lock and key.

"Shall we go up? . . . Lead the way, will you, Superintendent? . . . You've been here before. . . ."

The stained-glass windows on the staircase threw splashes of color on their faces as they passed, making them suddenly blood-red, then gold. Maigret rang. A hurried step inside; then the door opened.

"Go in, gentlemen," said Maigret, standing aside.

"Come in," echoed Madame Le Cloaguen.

What was the matter? She was nervous; there was something not quite natural in her manner as she showed them into the living room.

Turning to Maigret, the only one she knew, she asked: "Where is he?"

"Who do you mean? . . . As you know, these gentlemen have come to examine your husband and report on his state of mind. . . . I know you got the notice, which the magistrate here sent around this morning."

"Was that it?"

"Really, madame! A man came at half past ten this morning from the Palais de Justice and delivered a . . ."

"An envelope, yes. But it was addressed to my husband."

"Do you mean to say you didn't open it? You have no idea what it contained?"

"I'm not in the habit of opening other people's letters. I left it in the hall. I'll show you. . . . There, on that table . . ."

She opened the door and pointed to an old table. On the floor underneath lay the yellow envelope of the Public Prosecutor's Office. It was empty.

"What happened?"

"I don't know. . . . My husband came in as usual for lunch. . . ."

"Did he read the letter?"

"He must have, since neither I nor my daughter opened it, and there's no one else here. . . . Our maid's on vacation, you see. . . ."

"Did he have lunch with you?"

"Yes. You can see for yourself."

She opened another door. The dining-room table was laid for three. Fruit and cheese were still on it.

"You see. . . . After lunch, Octave disappeared, and I thought he'd gone to have a nap in his room. He spends a lot of time in his room, you know. He has a very retiring disposition. . . ."

She was not afraid of irony! She was talking about a man who was constantly kept out of the way and even locked in his room like a naughty schoolboy.

"Is he there now?"

"No. I looked in to see, just before you came. Then I noticed that his overcoat was gone from the hall. I thought he'd gone out again."

"What time was it when you last saw him?"

"We got up from the table at a quarter to one. . . . We always have lunch at the same time. . . . But would you tell me what these gentlemen . . ."

Maigret gave the examining magistrate a rueful smile. As for Madame Le Cloaguen, she had recovered her confidence.

"What surprises me is that you should ask me these questions. You ought to know better than I where he is, since our building is under observation from morning till night, and from night till morning."

The superintendent went to the window and, peering at the sidewalk opposite, saw Janvier, who was picking his teeth while he watched the building.

The two psychiatrists were rather put out. Since there was nobody for them to examine, they suggested they might as well return to their other work.

The examining magistrate looked crestfallen.

"Are you quite sure," he asked, "that he's nowhere in the apartment?"

And she, haughty as usual, replied: "Why don't you search the place while you're here? I don't know what you're waiting for."

A quarter of an hour later, they had found nothing. *Octave Le Cloaguen, his overcoat and hat, had vanished.*

7

No, Monsieur Magistrate, Maigret is not trying to rub it in! He isn't angry and he isn't sulking. The simple truth is that he's worried. There's a weight on his shoulders, all the heavier now that he feels he is beginning to understand. That's why he keeps so obstinately silent.

Unlike the superintendent, the examining magistrate couldn't keep his mouth shut for a moment. But then, he wasn't beginning to understand! In fact, it was just because he felt himself completely wrong that he was so talkative.

Maigret no longer saw the assurance of that morning, the self-satisfaction with which the magistrate had announced the measures he had taken.

But one must not confuse the police with choirboys. . . .

"Look here, Maigret . . . Only a madman would choose to live in a room like this. . . . It stands to reason. . . ."

Why should the old ship's doctor be mad? In his thirty-odd years with the police, Maigret had seen so many others who were madder; he'd sniffed the odor of human passions, of vices, of crimes, of mania, but here . . . ?

"It's not as if he was poor. He has a comfortable apartment, if not luxurious. And he stows himself away in a room little better than a kennel!"

No response from Maigret.

The psychiatrists had left, after handshakes all around,

leaving the examining magistrate to cope, which he did by fussing and expostulating. Madame Le Cloaguen and her daughter sat waiting in the living room, trying to guess, no doubt, what question they would be asked next.

The magistrate sent for Inspector Janvier, who was on watch below.

"Look here, my friend, are you sure you never lost sight of the entrance for a moment?"

"Only for ten or fifteen minutes, soon after the old man went in. I had to telephone the PJ to make my report."

"Well, you shouldn't have. . . . If you have to telephone, you must manage as best you can – I'm not concerned with that. But when you're told to watch a building, you must watch it, never take your eyes off it."

Maigret didn't even smile. All that was of no importance.

"I suppose you've had the curiosity to ask whether the house has any other exit?"

"There isn't one, Monsieur Magistrate."

"I have no doubt in my own mind, Maigret, that Le Cloaguen slipped out while your man's back was turned. Still, in a case as serious as this, we have no right to rule out other possibilities. You'd better send your inspector to find out whether Le Cloaguen is hiding in any of the other apartments. . . . Remember, you have no search warrant. I can't give you one now. Just ask if they'll let you have a look around."

Maigret said nothing. He simply stood there with his hands in his pockets staring at the floor. He had even let his pipe go out.

Waiting for Janvier, the magistrate began to lose his composure. When the inspector returned, it was to say there was no sign of the missing man.

"He has got to be found! He has got to be found! . . . Just think, Maigret. There's a madman at large in the streets of Paris, a homicidal maniac, who has already committed a murder. . . ."

He called to Madame Le Cloaguen.

"Tell me, madame, has your husband any money with him?"

"No."

"Are you sure?"

"Quite."

"You hear that, Maigret? He has no money on him! But he must eat. He must sleep somewhere. You see what I'm driving at? How is he going to get hold of some money? You follow my thought? . . . Can you give me a photograph of your husband, madame?"

Still Maigret said nothing, and the room seemed to be filled with his silence. The examining magistrate was ready to clutch at any straw. The photograph would be as good as any. It would be reproduced and circulated to the police all over the country. It would be published in the papers and seen by millions of readers. . . .

"I don't know of any photographs of my husband."

"Come! It doesn't need to be a studio portrait. It doesn't need to be a recent one. . . . You must have something. A passport photograph? . . ."

"My husband hasn't been out of the country for the last thirty years. Before that, he must have had a passport, but I've never seen it. If you didn't find it in his room, I think it must not exist."

The magistrate looked at Maigret, but he probably didn't even notice that the latter's eyes had lit up for a second. Certainly he didn't understand the meaning. If he had, he'd have stopped buzzing around.

"Maigret, would you call Missing Persons right away and give them a description of Octave Le Cloaguen? Tell them to . . ."

Yes, of course. Maigret would do everything that was

wanted. Mechanically. He was on the track of the truth, which lay, not in the streets of Paris or at the frontiers, but much nearer home.

He walked over to the telephone, which was attached to the wall in the hall. As he did so, he could feel Madame Le Cloaguen's gaze fixed on him, and out of the corner of his eye he could see Gisèle sitting there, and he recalled . . .

He recalled the old man's hands in the taxi when he had brought him back to Boulevard des Batignolles, those hands that trembled, the beads of sweat on the forehead. . . .

He could remember the exact moment when he noticed those symptoms. There had been no sign of them at the Police Judiciaire. None whatever. They had appeared only as the old man *drew near his own home.*

He hadn't shown any sign of fear in the apartment on Rue Caulaincourt in spite of the blood and the presence of a corpse.

And yesterday he had seemed positively relieved at the prospect of being arrested.

"Hello! . . . Missing Persons? . . . Is that you, Maniu? . . . Here's a description for you. Will you take it down and circulate it? . . . Yes, as widely as possible . . . The man must be handled carefully. . . . Yes. The examining magistrate is most particular about that. He's to be posted as extremely dangerous. . . ."

At the other end of the line Maniu chuckled; he knew exactly what Maigret thought of examining magistrates when they intervened in criminal investigations.

"Has he slipped through your fingers?"

"*Apparently* . . ."

The woman was standing just behind him. When he hung up, he turned around and looked straight into her eyes with such intensity that she couldn't repress a nervous twitch.

"I shudder to think," said the examining magistrate as they left the building, "yes, I positively shudder to think of that man's being at large – armed, in all probability, and ready for anything, to save his skin. You must admit, Maigret, it was most unfortunate that your man thought fit to absent himself like that. Just to telephone a mere formal report . . . We had the murderer in our hands! . . . There's no use telling me he didn't do it. The man who runs away is always guilty. . . . And now . . . are you going back to the Quai des Orfèvres?"

"I don't know."

"What are you going to do next?"

"I don't know yet."

"It's stopped you, hasn't it?"

What was the use of undeceiving him? Once again, Maigret said nothing. Nor did he say anything when Janvier, subdued and penitent, joined him on the sidewalk. It was not until they were drinking a beer on the terrace of the little restaurant across the street that he murmured: "Don't worry about it, old fellow."

"Still, if he makes a big noise . . ."

"He's made all the noise he's going to."

"Have you got an idea?"

No answer. Maigret filled his pipe in silence, lit it, then gazed at the dead match he was holding.

"I wonder if I have time," he said at last, with a sigh, stretching out his legs like a man who's very tired.

"Time for what, Chief?"

"To go to Saint-Raphaël."

"Can't you send somebody?"

No, that was just what he couldn't do. You can give an inspector a specific job, but you can't send him to the other end of the country just to have a look, to sniff around like a dog at a garbage can, to discover the bone, or whatever it might be, the secret they were looking for. . . .

Suddenly Maigret came to life. A curtain had moved in one of the windows opposite. A woman's eyes were trained on the superintendent. They were full of terror.

The next moment the face was gone. Maigret had seen it, however, and its effect on him was galvanic. He jumped to his feet.

"Come on. Let's get to work. . . . First of all, I want you to go up and stand outside the Le Cloaguens' apartment. Never mind if they see you."

"If the old girl comes out? . . . Just stay there?"

"Let her go. Don't move on any account!"

He watched Janvier cross the street, then went into the restaurant.

"Have you got a telephone?"

It was in the restaurant itself and not closed off. But Maigret did not care who heard him.

"Is that you, Lucas? . . . What did you say? . . . No. It's not important. If it pleases the Prosecutor's Office . . . Now, look . . . Jump in a taxi and join me here. . . . Yes, Boulevard des Batignolles. The little restaurant opposite. I'll be waiting for you."

The landlord looked at him with curiosity, wondering what had brought the police to the neighborhood, for of course he had understood.

"Mademoiselle, give me Saint-Raphaël, please. I don't know the number. They'll have to look it up down there. I want to speak to Maître Larignan. He's a lawyer, but that's all I know about him. . . . Police priority . . ."

It was obviously going to be a beer day. There were four empty bottles on his table by the time he got through to Saint-Raphaël.

"Hello! . . . No. This is the maid. . . . No, monsieur . . . Yes, monsieur . . . No, monsieur . . . Monsieur's out. . . .

What? . . .Yes, he's out. He must be on the jetty, painting. . . . Who's speaking? . . . Oh! the police! . . . Yes, monsieur, I'll go at once. . . ."

Maigret could imagine her rushing out of a clean white villa into the fierce sunlight of the Côte d'Azur, where the blue sea was dotted with sails, to find the amateur painter who had set up his easel on the jetty and was no doubt surrounded by a little group of curious onlookers.

"What'll you have, Lucas? . . . Landlord, two beers."

Lucas had realized at once that it wasn't the moment to ask questions. They sat at a table saying little, waiting for Maître Larignan to call, while Janvier sat on the top step of a flight of stairs, feeling very conspicuous and rather undignified, and jumping to his feet every time one of the tenants passed. The best part of an hour had elapsed before the telephone rang.

"Monsieur Larignan? . . . What's that? . . . No, monsieur, your wife hasn't met with an accident. I didn't even know she was in Paris. . . . Oh, she isn't? In Vichy for her liver? . . . That's good. . . . Tell me about a client of yours, Monsieur Le Cloaguen . . . Octave Le Cloaguen. . . . Yes, that's it. . . . Now, can you tell me at what date he stopped signing the receipts for the money you pay him? . . . I know all about it. There's nothing to be afraid of. . . . Why am I telephoning from a restaurant if I belong to the police? . . . Because I haven't got time to go back to the Quai des Orfèvres. . . . You're very much on your guard, Monsieur Larignan, but I assure you it's quite all right. . . . Ah! That's better. About ten years ago . . . An accident to his finger . . . In other words, at the same time the family left Saint-Raphaël for Paris . . . ?"

Maigret mopped his brow. There was no doubt about it: Maître Larignan was cautious, precise. The answers had to be dragged out of him word by word, and that was always difficult over the telephone.

"How was the annuity of two hundred thousand francs paid to him? . . . I see. You come to Paris every year and hand the money over. In bills? . . . Don't cut me off, mademoiselle. Listen in if it amuses you, but for the love of God don't cut me off. . . . Are you there, Monsieur Larignan? . . . Yes, I got that. You pay him in person. . . . What? . . . I understand. It was stipulated in the will. . . . Of course . . . Yes . . . Yes."

The Saint-Raphaël lawyer was one of those people who think you have to shout into the telephone for a long-distance call. In a bellowing voice he explained that it was his duty to make sure each year that Monsieur Le Cloaguen was still alive.

"So you've seen him every year. How was he? . . . In bed? . . . No? . . . Always more or less ill, but never in bed . . . I see. . . . Thinner and thinner . . . Go on. Don't be afraid. . . . Yes . . . Really? . . . It's strange, certainly. . . . You found him odd. Not exactly mad, but eccentric? . . . At his age, of course. . . . Just one more thing. The villa they occupied? Empty at the moment? . . . Rented to an American woman who hasn't come to France for two or three years? You have the keys? . . . Well, will you please hand them to the person I'll be sending? . . . You needn't worry. I'll have a search warrant telegraphed from the Public Prosecutor's Office. Thank you very much, Monsieur Larignan. I'd be glad if you'd stay within easy reach in case I have to call you again. . . ."

"A beer, landlord!"

Maigret looked much happier when he rejoined Lucas on the terrace. There was even a hint of a smile.

"Very funny! . . . You'd never guess what's been going

on. One day, when Monsieur Larignan went to pay the annuity, he saw a grammar book. And Madame Le Cloaguen seemed to have been giving her husband a lesson. 'I'm glad to see you're studying,' Monsieur Larignan joked. He was startled to find he'd said the wrong thing."

"I don't get the point."

"Wait! . . . You'll see it before the evening is out. . . . Now I must call our friend the examining magistrate, who's going to send me to the devil."

The little restaurant had become a sort of police headquarters. It was as though Maigret couldn't bear the thought of losing sight of that big gray building, in one of whose windows a curtain quivered from time to time.

"Hello! . . . I'm sorry to bother you, Magistrate. . . . No. Nothing of any importance . . . But I'd like you to telegraph an order to Saint-Raphaël. . . ."

Maigret gave Maître Larignan's address and that of the villa that was to be searched.

"They must take a mason with them and one or two bricklayers. . . . Dangerous? . . . Yes. I know. The owner will make a row when he finds out. . . . Never mind. I assure you it's necessary. . . . Yes, the whole place. The cellars, the garden, the well, if there is one – everything, absolutely everything. . . . I'd like them to report the result to me here. . . . Thank you, Magistrate."

Was it the fifth or sixth glass of beer? Little by little Maigret had become another man. Not that it was the effect of the beer. He was going into action, so to speak, and all his faculties were mobilized. He seemed to be driving steadily forward with calm relentlessness.

"Anything I can do, Chief?" asked Lucas.

"See if you can get an evening paper."

There it was already – the description of Octave Le Cloaguen:

A dangerous madman who is believed to have murdered the fortuneteller of Rue Caulaincourt is at this moment loose on the streets of the capital.

Maigret shrugged his shoulders. If that's what the examining magistrate wanted, he could have it! Anyhow, it served to amuse the public and keep the reporters happy.

"Do you think he's run away?"

"No."

"In that case . . . ?"

"Well . . . perhaps he has, perhaps he hasn't."

"And the two women?"

"Never mind them. Let's go. . . . Landlord, how much is all this? If any call comes for me, either from Saint-Raphaël or the Quai des Orfèvres, ask them to hold the line and come get me, from the building across the street."

Really he'd rather have waited. He had the feeling that the whole case was going to open up quickly. But there was the question of Le Cloaguen. Where was he? Was he alive or dead? The answer couldn't wait.

They crossed the street, and Maigret knocked on the concierge's door.

"Good afternoon, madame. Yes, it's me again. . . . Tell me, does each tenant have a locked area in the cellar? . . . Would you mind taking us down there? . . . A flashlight? Yes. Thanks. You might as well bring one. . . ."

They went down one behind the other. The huge vaulted cellar was divided into cubicles, with partitions made of rough unplaned boards, and in them were heaps of coal, old boxes, and so on. They came to the Le Cloaguens' cubicle.

"No, you needn't bother the ladies. It's a very simple lock; we can deal with it in no time."

It was indeed only a matter of seconds before the door was opened. Inside were some empty bags that had contained potatoes, a pile of recently delivered logs, the remains of last winter's coal.

"Have you a shovel, madame?"

"You'll get dirty."

Never mind if he did! He patiently shoveled the coal aside until it was quite clear there was nothing beneath. Then, with the same patience, he checked the cubicles of the other tenants.

"What about the maids' rooms? I suppose the Le Cloaguens have one or two, judging by the size of their apartment."

"On the seventh floor. Yes, they have two."

"May we see them?"

"If you'll just wait while I go turn my gas down. Otherwise my ragout will be burned."

Janvier got to his feet to let them pass and mournfully watched them climb to the floor above.

"We were going to have an elevator put in, but it wasn't possible because the stairwell is too narrow."

After the last flight of stairs, the scene changed abruptly. With no attempt to maintain appearances there was a long, badly lighted corridor with numbered doors on either side.

"Here we are: 13 and 14 . . . Last year they tried to rent one, but they asked for so much that nobody would look at it. . . . I have a passkey."

Lucas, who had followed the other two, was beginning to feel uneasy. In Number 13 there was such a musty smell that it caught them by the throat. It contained a child's crib, a couple of broken chairs, and a box with a miscellaneous assortment of books.

"You see, they only use it to store a few things that might just as well be thrown away."

Number 14 was much the same. A globe, a dressmaker's

dummy, and more books, mostly medical, and some fly-blown anatomical charts.

"You see . . . they're both empty. . . ."

"Yes. They're empty," said Maigret like an echo.

Yet he seemed unable to tear himself away from that corridor that led nowhere.

"One more question, madame . . . Why is there a ladder at the top of the stairs?"

"Oh, that thing! I'd like to be rid of it, since it's never used. But, you see, there's a sort of attic over the last three rooms. To get to it you need a ladder."

"Is there anything up there?"

"Well, certain tenants are allowed to store big trunks there, but, to tell the truth, I've never been up to see."

A glance at Lucas, who went obediently to get the ladder.

"Shall I go up, Chief?"

"No."

Maigret was going up himself, and Lucas couldn't help feeling uncomfortable.

"You'd better take this with you, Chief."

Lucas held out his revolver, which the superintendent accepted with a shrug of the shoulders.

The ladder bent under Maigret's weight so much that he changed his mind and came down again.

"He can't be dead," he murmured.

"Why not?"

"Because I defy a couple of women to hoist a body up that ladder."

He raised his head, as one might to call a boy down from a tree.

"Le Cloaguen!" he called. "Le Cloaguen!"

Silence. The concierge was so affected that she put her hand to her heart, as though to be ready for more surprises.

"Listen, old fellow, I hate ladders, and this one isn't fit to bear my weight. You might as well save me the trouble. . . ."

Silence.

"Very well, then! I'm to come up?"

A faint sound. Someone moved up there. Someone bumped against a hollow object, no doubt an empty trunk. Then a leg came in sight. A foot hovered in the air feeling for a rung of the ladder. Finally a man in a greenish overcoat came down, step by step.

No one could have imagined the triumphant joy Maigret felt at that moment. Yes, one man, Lucas, who knew his chief well, and could have sworn there were tears in his eyes.

As a rule, Maigret took his successes calmly, but this time he couldn't help being pleased. He had worked things out by himself, with nothing to guide him but the most fragmentary clues, his own intuition, and his capacity for putting himself in other people's shoes.

"You're lucky, Le Cloaguen!"

The old man showed no fear now. He stood there passively, like a man who has done his best and is now resigned to whatever may be in store for him. His only reaction was a faint sigh, which might easily have been a sigh of relief.

"If we hadn't come, I think you might have died of hunger. . . ."

The old man didn't seem to understand, but, after hesitating, he asked: "Have you arrested them?"

He was covered with dust and cobwebs. The space above was not high enough for a man to stand.

"Have you arrested them?" What that question meant was: My wife and daughter were going to bring me food. If not, it could only mean they were no longer there.

Lucas was still gazing at his chief in admiration.

"No," said Maigret. "I haven't arrested them. Not yet."

Le Cloaguen looked at him with surprise.

"Never mind! You'll see in a moment. Come along."

They all went down the stairs. Once again Janvier jumped to his feet. Maigret pointed to him.

"You see this man, Le Cloaguen? . . . With him here, they'd never have dared bring you any food. . . . It was why I was obliged to act today, why I couldn't wait."

They could hear creeping footsteps on the other side of the front door. Maigret rang.

"You can go now, madame," he said to the concierge. "Many thanks for your help."

The door opened a few inches. A pointed nose. A foxy face. The sharp eyes of Madame Le Cloaguen. A cry.

"Oh! So you've found him! . . . Where was he?"

"Come in, Lucas. Come in, Janvier. You too, old man."

Le Cloaguen started at Maigret's familiar tone. The superintendent had never spoken to him like that before. It seemed to please him, to reassure him.

"We're not going to do anything to you. We're not going to make you recite the rules for past participles!"

This time it was the woman who started. She turned on Maigret as if she'd been stung.

"What do you mean by that?"

"Just what I said, madame . . . Lucas, don't let this woman out of your sight. Janvier, go and get the daughter. Same thing with her."

He turned to Le Cloaguen.

"We don't need to bother about you, do we? You're not going to give us any more trouble. . . ."

"Can I take off my overcoat?" he asked.

"Of course."

Maigret watched the operation with keen interest. It was as though he expected some extraordinary revelation. It turned out, however, to be nothing very spectacular. One shoulder of the coat must have been unusually padded, because without it the old man had one shoulder noticeably lower than the other.

Lucas and Janvier saw Maigret's eyes twinkle, but they were at a loss why. The superintendent knocked out his pipe, took his spare one from his pocket and filled it.

There were six of them in the somberly furnished green-curtained room. The hum of Paris traffic reached them from below. They stood as still as waxworks, except for Madame Le Cloaguen, who kept clasping and unclasping her hands.

There were hurried steps outside, on the stairs, which hesitated at the door. Maigret walked calmly across the hall and opened it.

"You're wanted on the telephone, Superintendent. . . . Saint-Raphaël."

The landlord of the little restaurant was disconcerted by the cold figures staring at him as though dumbfounded.

Before going, Maigret looked back from the door.

"Look here, ladies . . ."

He paused and stared hard at Madame Le Cloaguen before going on.

"If there's any trouble at all . . ."

And he cheerfully tapped his revolver pocket.

"I'll be back in a few minutes."

8

From the point of view of the public, this was far from being one of Maigret's most resounding successes. For, after giving it a lot of publicity, the papers suddenly stopped talking about the fortuneteller of Rue Caulaincourt. Nor was there any further mention of the homicidal maniac supposed to be at large. At the Quai des Orfèvres, on the other hand, it was long remembered, and one remark made in the course of that evening was so often quoted that it became part of PJ tradition.

At about five, a heavy thunderstorm broke over Paris, after more than four weeks of heat and drought.

"I don't think I'd ever seen anything like it," Lucas was never tired of saying.

They had remained in the room with the green curtains. Lucas and Janvier on one side, the two women on the other, the old man off to one side.

Maigret had been gone about twenty minutes, and Madame Le Cloaguen was finding the suspense more and more difficult to bear. Finally she got up from her chair and went and stood by the window, one hand gripping a curtain, in the way she had spent much of the day, watching the inspectors on duty below.

Then the storm came. First of all, a gust of wind that swept the dust of the street right up to the fourth-floor windows and made the awning of the little restaurant flap like the sails of a boat. Then the rain, sheets of it. The taxis driving past made ripples almost like the bow wave of a boat. In a few seconds, every pedestrian had dived into the nearest shelter, and the sidewalks were deserted.

The living room grew darker, until the only thing lighted clearly was Madame Le Cloaguen's face at the window. Lucas was gazing at it, ruminating on the horrible fate of marrying such a woman, when she turned around abruptly.

"Where's he going?" she asked angrily, pointing down toward the street.

Maigret had just emerged from the little restaurant and, turning up his jacket collar, was hurrying toward Place Clichy, presumably in search of a taxi.

It was then that she made the remark that was to become famous around the Police Judiciaire.

"I hope he hasn't forgotten us!"

Lucas, who had conscientiously modeled himself on Maigret, calmly filled his pipe. Then he remembered that the old man chewed tobacco, and handed him his pouch.

"Can I get something from my room?" whispered the old man, his eyes shining.

In spite of what Maigret had said, Lucas thought it wiser to accompany him.

The old man rummaged in a cupboard, finally producing an old sock, from which he took a pipe with a broken stem.

"They can't stop me now, can they?"

Holding Lucas's pouch in his hand, he walked with childish glee back into the living room, where he sat down again and began filling his pipe. He did it very slowly, to prolong the pleasure, before striking a match from the box the sergeant gave him.

Madame Le Cloaguen looked more venomous than ever, but all she said was: "I really can't see why there's any need to keep us waiting like this. . . ."

Yet her troubles were only just starting. The minutes passed. A loose shutter rattled against the outside wall. The rain beat down relentlessly, but a few people plucked up their courage and made a dash through it. The room filled gradually with clouds of tobacco smoke.

Over an hour had gone by when a taxi drew up outside. Three minutes later, there were steps on the stairs and a ring at the bell. Janvier opened the door.

"Oh, it's you, Monsieur Magistrate . . . Come in. . . . No, he's not here. . . . He went to telephone across the street. The last we saw of him he was hurrying off toward Place Clichy."

The examining magistrate, who had brought a tall, thin man with him, bowed rather awkwardly to the two women. He knew nothing of what had happened. He had merely received an urgent message from Maigret requesting him to come to Boulevard des Batignolles, with his clerk.

The living room, dark at the best of times, was now bathed in a twilight gloom, broken occasionally by a flash of lightning, which made them all jump. Little was said. They sat there eyeing each other in silence like people in a doctor's waiting room. The old man puffed blissfully at his foul pipe, which he kept replenishing with Lucas's tobacco.

Janvier looked at his watch, and from then on that was about the only thing they could find to do. A little later, it was the examining magistrate's turn, then his clerk's, then Janvier's again.

Seven o'clock . . . Half past . . . And suddenly the silence was broken by the voice of Octave Le Cloaguen, who turned to Lucas to say rather shyly: "There's a bottle of port in the sideboard. . . . *But she's got the key. . . .*"

A flash of hatred as Madame Le Cloaguen, without a word, took a key from her bag and put it on the table.

"A glass of port, madame?"

"No, thank you."

Her daughter, less able to stand the strain, murmured: "Just a little, please. Half a glass . . ."

At eight o'clock Lucas switched on the light, but it was such a poor one that the room looked almost as murky as before. He and Janvier were both hungry, but there seemed little prospect of a meal.

At last the bell rang. This time it was Lucas who answered it. When Maigret's voice was heard from the landing outside, he was saying in his most urbane tones: "Come in, will you, madame?"

A little old lady, dressed very neatly in black, hesitated at the door, then came forward rather timidly. Her cheeks were fresh, and she was remarkably well preserved for her age. She held her bag in front of her with both hands and seemed surprised to find so many people there. Then her eyes fell on Madame Le Cloaguen.

She didn't hold out her hand, but in a stilted voice that betrayed a host of old resentments she said: "Good evening, Antoinette."

Maigret's clothes were as shiny as a wet umbrella, and he left a trail of drops on the polished parquet floor. He nodded to the examining magistrate and his clerk, but made no explanation.

"If this kind gentleman hadn't insisted, I'd never have come. Not after . . ."

She broke off, having caught sight of the old man. She opened her mouth to speak, but no sound came from it. She screwed up her eyes, then fumbled in her bag and took out a pair of spectacles.

She seemed quite at a loss. It was as though she felt herself the victim of some practical joke. She looked at Maigret, then at Antoinette Le Cloaguen, then once more at the old man.

He stared back at her blankly, unable to understand why she was so interested in him.

"But . . . but that's not my brother! That's not Octave! . . . My God! And to think that I have been wondering all these years why he . . ."

"Sit down, madame. . . . Magistrate, let me introduce Madame Biron, now a widow, who was formerly Mademoiselle Catherine Le Cloaguen. It was only this afternoon that I learned of her existence, from the Saint-Raphaël police. . . . Do sit down, madame. And don't worry about the canon, for we won't keep you here long. . . .

"You see, Magistrate, Madame Biron was left in straitened circumstances when her husband died. He was a good man, who worked at the town hall in Saint-Denis. Madame Biron is now employed as housekeeper by an old bedridden canon, whom she was most reluctant to leave even for half an hour. . . .

"Now tell us about your brother, Octave, Madame Biron."

The two sisters-in-law looked at each other defiantly, yet when Madame Biron began to speak, she did so with hesitation and with a quietness that was perhaps a reflection of the ecclesiastical surroundings in which she now lived.

"Our parents were not rich. In fact, it was all they could do to make their son a doctor. . . . He went to sea, as you probably know, and in the course of his travels had the good fortune to win the gratitude of a very rich man. . . . With the annuity he was given, he retired, got married, and settled down in Saint-Raphaël, but even with a family of his own, he was always generous to us. . . ."

"Excuse me . . . Do you mean that he regularly gave you money?"

"Regularly, no . . . My husband would hardly have liked that. But he seized on every pretext for giving us a present or helping in some way. . . . Fifteen years ago, when I had a bad attack of bronchitis, he insisted on my staying in his house, though it wasn't long before I realized I wasn't wanted!"

A meaning look at Madame Le Cloaguen.

"I think Octave noticed it too, only he didn't like to say anything. . . . You see . . . Well, I think he often regretted the time he'd spent away at sea. . . . He bought a small boat, because he was very fond of fishing, at sea, all alone. It was the only way for him to get a little peace."

"Did they live comfortably?"

"Yes, I think so. . . . They always had servants. Two, if I remember right. . . ."

"In other words they lived as people live who have an income of two hundred thousand francs a year?"

"I daresay. . . . But I've never had that much money myself, so I really don't know."

"Did your brother have good health?"

"Yes. So far as I know. I can't remember his ever being really ill. . . . What's happened to him?"

Everyone looked at Madame Le Cloaguen, who sat, very tense, with her lips pursed.

"Would it have been to your sister-in-law's advantage to get rid of him?"

"You don't mean . . . ? As a matter of fact, I think she had every reason to keep him alive as long as possible, because the annuity, if I'm not mistaken, was payable only during his lifetime."

"Have you anything to tell us, Madame Le Cloaguen?"

She answered merely with a look of such fury that Maigret couldn't help smiling.

"Very well!" he said. "Then, Magistrate, I'll have to do the explaining. But first of all, what have you been drinking?"

"Port . . . Like a glass?"

Maigret made a face.

"If that's the best you can do."

Again the old man intervened.

"There's a half-bottle of cognac in *her* room."

In *her* room, of course!

"Well, here's the story. . . . The Le Cloaguens were leading at Saint-Raphaël the easy, comfortable lives of well-to-do people. I've had a word, over the phone, with the bank there. . . . Ten years ago, Dr. Le Cloaguen had a balance of barely fifty thousand francs, and as far as is known that was the sum total of his savings. . . . And then he suddenly died. . . . Perhaps sometime his widow will make up her mind to tell us what he died of. . . . Perhaps a sudden stroke . . .

"Be that as it may, his wife and daughter found themselves faced with poverty. And there are people who will go to any lengths to avoid poverty. . . .

"By chance, they had seen an elderly tramp wandering along the quays in Cannes, a simple-minded and quite harmless individual, whose resemblance to Dr. Le Cloaguen was striking. . . ."

The old man smiled benignly, not in the least offended by the description of himself.

"Late this afternoon, the Saint-Raphaël police, acting under our instructions, found the remains of the true Octave Le Cloaguen walled up in a recess in the cellar of the villa where he'd lived.

"There you are! . . . There's only one more detail. The women had little difficulty persuading the old tramp to exchange his precarious and even miserable existence for one of comfort and security under another name. But there was one serious obstacle. What about the receipts for the annuity payments? They had to be signed, and the old man couldn't manage to imitate the dead man's signature. It was all he could do to write his own name. . . .

"So he had to have an accident to his right forefinger. And that was a sufficient reason for him not to sign.

"Even though the resemblance between the two men was remarkable, it was too dangerous to remain on the Côte d'Azur. So they came to Paris.

"There was also the doctor's sister, who was not likely to be fooled. Steps were taken to offend her so deeply that she would never come near her brother and his family again."

"That person," murmured Madame Biron, "as much as told me I was a beggar. I wrote to my brother, but he never answered. . . . Now I understand. . . ."

"Money! . . ." Maigret said. "Money! The whole affair is a question of money. The sordidness of it! For the sake of money she denied her husband a decent burial. . . .

"The tramp was a bit slimmer than Dr. Le Cloaguen, so he was condemned to wear an overcoat both winter and summer. One of his shoulders drooped, so the coat was padded. He was almost illiterate, so he was made to study grammar. I'd guess he wasn't very successful, for in the end they thought it best to say he'd gone weak in the head, owing to a stroke he'd had years ago in the Far East. . . ."

With a disgusted expression on his face, the superintendent looked around the room.

"It would be a little less repugnant if they'd made some use of this money. But no. The second Octave Le Cloaguen might die like the first, and there was no hope of finding another substitute. So they began, with absolute avarice, to save every franc they could, living with such miserly economy that they have in the last ten years saved over a million and a half. . . . Am I right, Madame Le Cloaguen? . . .

"As for you, Picard . . ."

The old man seemed to be touched by the sound of his real name.

"You sold your birthright for a mess of pottage. . . . You have a bed, admittedly. You have food, since you have to be kept alive. But that's about all. No smoking, no drinking, because Dr. Le Cloaguen neither smoked nor drank. Besides, those things cost money! . . . You are like a dog on a leash. Your only distraction is to wander through the streets, a pastime that costs nothing. . . . Every year, when the lawyer comes to see you, you're said to be ill, and he is merely given a glimpse of you in your room, which is kept as dark as possible. . . .

"You managed nevertheless to escape the vigilance of your jailers. You managed nevertheless to keep a secret from them right to the end."

Picard turned his head away. There were tears in his eyes.

"From a marriage long ago, you had a daughter. . . . You found her again in Paris, where she was a fortuneteller . . . Mademoiselle Jeanne of Rue Caulaincourt."

In the murky atmosphere of that room, the faces were rather like paintings in a dingy old museum. Maigret was silent. The examining magistrate, ill at ease, crossed his legs, uncrossed them again, then cleared his throat.

"Madame Le Cloaguen," he asked, "did you kill Mademoiselle Jeanne?"

"It's not true!"

"Madame Le Cloaguen, did you follow your husband, your supposed husband, to Rue Caulaincourt, and did you enter Number 67 *bis*?"

"It's not true," she repeated.

"Do you admit disposing of your husband's body in the cellar of your villa at Saint-Raphaël?"

"And if I did?"

"Do you admit fraudulently drawing an annuity to which you were not entitled?"

"I do not. . . . The money was always paid to this man here, not to me. If this man handed it over to me, I had every right to take it."

"My God! My God!" stammered the canon's housekeeper, aghast.

Even the men, who had seen plenty of tough customers in their time, looked at each other with something like bewilderment when Madame Le Cloaguen went on.

"You know exactly what I face. So do I. A fine not exceeding fifty francs and a term of imprisonment not exceeding two months. Article 368 of the Penal Code!"

Yes, she had it all at her fingertips. She was pleased with herself. Her lips quivered slightly, but it was a quiver of triumph.

"I had no idea that this man had ever been married or had a daughter. I had no idea he ever visited anyone when he went out for his walks. . . . As for my husband, I can't see what difference it made to him whether he lay in a cemetery or a cellar. . . ."

"Shame on you!" burst out Madame Biron, unable to contain herself any longer. "Can't you see what a monster you are? Never would I have believed that any of God's creatures could have said a thing like that! . . . When I think of my poor brother . . . Superintendent, I can't bear it. I can hardly breathe. Can't we have a window open?"

Indeed, she had turned quite pale, and there were beads of sweat on her upper lip. Maigret opened a window, and a gust of damp air blew through the green curtains and swept through the stuffy room.

"And now, Maigret?" asked the examining magistrate. It seemed to him that the superintendent had lost some of his usual assurance. He smoked his pipe and paced up and down, finally coming to a halt right in front of Madame Le Cloaguen, at whom he stared with all the force at his command. His face was hard as stone.

"You're right, madame. . . . The law of the land is powerless to treat you as you deserve. . . . Yet, in the whole course of my career, I don't think I've ever seen any human being sink quite so low for the sake of money. I think I would have more respect for you if you'd killed your husband in a fit of passion. . . ."

A little cry from Madame Biron.

"I'm sorry, madame, but I simply had to speak my mind. . . . The examining magistrate asked you just now, Madame Le Cloaguen, whether you killed Mademoiselle Jeanne. You say you didn't, and I believe you. But I know very well that if you cared to speak, you could in a moment put us on the track of the person who did. Am I wrong?"

She studied him from head to foot. For a second she hesitated. Then the expression on her face grew even harder, if that was possible.

"No!" she said.

"In that case . . ."

"I shall tell you nothing. Do you hear?"

Suddenly she was transformed. She lost her self-control. Now she was a fury.

"Never!" she screamed. "Never! I won't tell you a thing. I hate all of you, and most of all this hulking bully, Superintendent Maigret. I hated him from the moment he set his clumsy feet in this apartment. . . . I hate you! I hate you! . . . You'll get nothing out of me. You'll never find out the truth. . . . I'll pay my fifty francs. . . . I'll serve my two months. . . . That's all! . . ."

"To whom did you pay two hundred thousand francs recently?"

"I will not tell you."

Then she changed her mind. Too late, however.

"What two hundred thousand francs?"

"The francs you drew out of the bank last Saturday."

No answer.

"Where did you go last Sunday between ten in the morning and four in the afternoon?"

She gave him a sneering look. Maigret felt sure her boast had not been a vain one. She was capable of holding out, and not even the most grueling interrogation would drag from her what she wished to keep back.

"Monsieur Magistrate, may I ask you to give me a warrant for the arrest of this woman and her daughter?"

"My daughter? What has she got to do with it? . . . Monsieur Magistrate, you know you have no right to do that. . . . I did not kill that woman, and the superintendent admits I did not. . . . And when I secretly buried my husband's body – and that's the only thing you've got against me – my daughter was not yet of age. She was a child, I tell you, and you have no right . . ."

It was already a melodrama and looked now as though it would degenerate into a farce. She was obviously the sort of woman who would defend herself with tooth and claw. Literally!

"I did not kill that woman. I never even knew of her existence."

"Who did it then?"

"I don't know. . . . I won't say another word. I hate you all. And you! You are a brute!"

The brute was, of course, Maigret, who turned away and poured himself another glass of port and mopped his brow. The examining magistrate was still looking at him with questioning eyes. He had thought for a moment the whole case was in the bag. Now he realized it was as delicate a problem as ever.

"Lucas, take the old woman away."

Maigret said that on purpose, and earned another devastating look.

"Janvier, take care of the daughter. . . . Look out!"

Madame Le Cloaguen had made a dash for the open window, but it was not, as the superintendent supposed, to throw herself out. She had lost all sense of proportion and leaned over the window sill screaming for help, as though there were burglars in the house, regardless of the fact that there wasn't a soul to hear her on Boulevard des Batignolles, which was still more like a river than a street.

"Handcuffs, Lucas . . . Janvier, shut the window."

A laugh, an uncanny, nervous laugh from the old tramp. It was too much for him, the sight of the woman who had browbeaten him for ten long years fighting furiously with the little sergeant. She was hitting out wildly, scratching, and kicking his shins. It couldn't last long, and soon she stood there, still panting, looking down at her handcuffed wrists.

The old man went off into another peal of strange laughter.

"Let me call my lawyer. I insist," Madame Le Cloaguen said. "You have no right. . . . Nobody has the right. . . ."

The juiciest part of the comedy was still to come, however. It came with a ring of the bell. Maigret opened the door.

"Excuse me . . . Is my friend . . . ?"

A middle-aged fussily dressed woman, followed by a tall, shy young man. . . . She glanced with surprise at the many strangers in the room. Then her eyes fell on Madame Le Cloaguen, and she started toward her, a delighted smile on her face.

"Antoinette! . . . How are you, my dear? . . . Would you believe it, this dreadful thunderstorm . . ."

She stopped dead. She had held out both her hands, but

those they were intending to grasp . . . It wasn't possible! . . . Handcuffs!

"But . . ."

She understood. These men must be policemen. And to think that she, a Cascurant de Nemours, had almost married her son to a . . .

"Come, Germain! This is no place for us. . . ."

Her astonishment had changed to anger. The whole thing was a trap. . . . Thank heavens there were no reporters or photographers! . . . If their name got into the papers . . .

"Disgraceful!" she muttered, and, dragging her son behind her, she ran down the stairs as fast as she could.

With his forefinger Maigret pressed down the tobacco in his pipe. One last look around, then a nod to Lucas and Janvier.

"Take them away."

The canon's housekeeper was afraid she'd be forgotten, but Maigret reassured her. No, he hadn't forgotten.

"As for you, madame, I'm going to take you home in a taxi, if you'll let me."

He couldn't have spoken more gently if she'd been his own mother.

9

The strange mixture of elements in Maigret's make-up came out strongly at moments like this. While his physical being reveled luxuriously in the delights of good food, his mind, detached from his surroundings, worked at a feverish pace.

In spite of the storm, it was a hot night, and the windows of the big brasserie on Boulevard Clichy were wide open. The two men were sitting at a table right in front, next to the terrace. On one side of them were the bright lights and the warm hum and bustle of waiters coming and going and diners chatting; on the other, deserted tables under the dripping awning, except for one, at which two prostitutes sat with empty glasses in front of them. Beyond that, the glistening sidewalk and the rain, which, though still persistent, was no longer the downpour they had seen earlier. On the other side of Place Blanche, with its neon lights reflected in the wet street, the illuminated sails of the Moulin Rouge turned unceasingly.

Gusts of damp air with a hint of autumn blew on their faces. The two men had finished their onion soup with grated cheese, and the waiter brought two plates heaped with *choucroute garnie* and two more glasses of beer. Snatches of music came to them from somewhere or other. As for the old tramp, his whole attention was focused on every mouthful, the aroma, the taste; he was enjoying each second of this memorable evening. From time to time, he raised his head to glance a little apologetically at the superintendent, as though to excuse himself.

It was midnight. Earlier, when Lucas was bundling the two women into the taxi, Maigret had held him by the sleeve.

"Where are you taking them?"

"To prison, as you said, Chief."

"No. Take them to our place and keep them till I get back. Janvier had better stay with you."

So the mother and daughter hadn't yet had to rub shoulders with the women brought in hourly by the vanload as raids against prostitutes were made in various districts. They now sat rigidly waiting in an empty office at the Quai des Orfèvres, and they carefully avoided uttering the least word for fear of giving something away. Only Antoinette Le Cloaguen's lips moved, like those of the old women in black you see kneeling by the pillars in a church, as she prepared the story she was going to tell her lawyer.

The little old lady, Madame Biron, had been taken back to her canon. On the way, she had turned to the superintendent in the taxi to say: "Is it possible that one of God's creatures could bring herself to do such things?"

That had left only the old man, whom Maigret had taken under his wing and was plying with soup and *choucroute garnie* till he was in seventh heaven.

"Did she starve you?"

"It was what you said – just enough to keep me alive. And in my room. Why I didn't die of hunger . . . The daughter wasn't nearly so bad. Sometimes she gave me something when her mother wasn't looking. . . ."

"Why didn't you walk out on them?"

The look the poor man gave Maigret answered the question before he spoke. It was the look of a man who has been kicked around all his life and has never had the strength to stand up for himself.

"You don't know her. . . . She's terrible. Sometimes I thought she was going to beat me. . . . Over and over again she said that if I ever told, she'd kill me. . . . You should have seen her when we were burying the corpse in Saint-Raphaël. She made me do it. . . . She helped me though – with her own hands, she did – working like a man. When we lugged the body down the stairs, she didn't turn a hair. It might have been a sack of potatoes for all she cared. . . ."

"Who killed your daughter, Picard?"

Maigret had let the old man finish his *choucroute* before asking the question. When he did, he spoke in a matter-of-fact, almost casual voice, while he gazed across the street at the flickering movements of the windmill.

"I can tell you one thing, Superintendent. It wasn't her. I swear it wasn't. . . . I don't know who did it. . . . If I did . . ."

His voice trailed off sadly. It was a shame to spoil this wonderful night by bringing up *that* again.

"Once, Marie told me . . . She was always Marie to me. Jeanne – that was only for the customers. . . . Once, she told me I shouldn't come see her just any time, but should drop her a line to say when I was coming. . . . But I went just the same. . . . I always waited outside for a while before going up, in case a customer came. . . . That day I didn't see anybody, and when I went up I found her alone."

The old man brought out his broken old pipe, foraged from God knew where. Maigret hesitated a moment; then without a word handed him one of his own, since he always carried two pipes in his pocket. The other filled it. Women at a neighboring table were laughing loudly. On the sidewalk outside, a man kept passing and repassing, trying in the dim light to make out which of the two prostitutes was the more desirable.

"She was worried. . . . She said she was in some sort of trouble. She wouldn't say what it was except that it had something to do with me and that it might turn out badly. . . . A car stopped outside, and she jumped up and looked down from the balcony. . . . It was then that she shoved me into the kitchen. I didn't hear her lock the door, but I suppose she must have. . . ."

"So you didn't see the man who came up?"

"No . . . I heard someone talking in a low voice."

"You're sure it was a man?"

"Yes . . . But I've just thought of another thing Marie said. . . . What was it? . . . I easily get mixed up. . . ."

Maigret ordered two glasses of brandy and waited patiently, puffing on his pipe.

"Oh, yes. I remember now. . . . She said she knew somebody who'd known me in Cannes, someone who came up to Paris every week and had spotted me one day leaving her place."

Maigret didn't show by a flicker of a muscle how much that information might mean to him. He took deep breaths of the cool air, as though it had the whole flavor of a Paris night, and while his eyes rested almost lovingly on the familiar things around him, other images rose in his mind with extraordinary clarity.

These were his great moments, and they more than compensated him for all the office work, the petty details, which made so many cases so boring.

Picard, the old tramp, roaming the streets and quays of Cannes . . .

"Tell me, Picard, how did you come to that?"

"I don't know . . . except that nothing I did ever went

right. . . . I was a packer in a shoe factory at Caen. . . . But my wife ran away – I never knew who with or where she went. . . . And then I got a job here and a job there. And whenever I felt like it, I took the train – it didn't matter where. . . . Then one day I stopped traveling. . . . It was in Cannes . . . When that woman . . ."

The old man's face changed. Obviously he would never shake off the feeling of terror she had instilled in him.

"I was getting old, you see . . . tired. . . . And the thought of a bed and regular meals . . ."

The naïve look came back into his eyes as he asked: "Do you think she really would have killed me?"

"I don't know, Picard, but I wouldn't put it past her."

Maigret mused. . . . Sidelights on poverty . . . An old man who's had enough of it sells himself into slavery for a little security. A woman who has never known it is so afraid of it that she sacrifices all that makes life worth living. Rather than face it, she would go to any lengths. . . .

Yes. To any lengths! . . .

"Well, it's time we went. Waiter! The check, please!"

All around them were people who were living their own lives. Maigret was living half a dozen lives at once. He was in Cannes, in Saint-Raphaël, in Morsang-sur-Seine, on Boulevard des Batignolles, Rue Caulaincourt, Place des Vosges . . .

They were all around him, in the rain.

The old man asked artlessly: "Where are we going?"

"Look here, Picard . . . would you mind, for just one night, sleeping in the jail?"

"Are they there?"

"No. Not yet. In any case, you wouldn't see them. . . . I'll get you out in the morning."

"All right . . . if you want . . ."

"Taxi! . . . To the Dépôt."

The dark quays. The red light over the entrance to the Dépôt.

"Good night, old fellow . . . I'll see you tomorrow. . . . Guard, take good care of this man, will you?"

The guard would have been surprised to learn that his charge had shortly before been having supper with Superintendent Maigret in a brasserie on Boulevard Clichy.

Only two windows were lighted up at the Quai des Orfèvres. Maigret could picture the two women sitting primly, Lucas yawning, and Janvier having no doubt just sent out for beer and sandwiches.

Should he go up? Maigret didn't want to. Instead, he walked along the quay, then stopped and leaned over the parapet to stare at the black river as fine rain cooled his forehead.

Thoughts flitted through his mind. . . . Of course! . . . The fortuneteller was expecting her fate, or at any rate something unpleasant. . . . She had spoken of a man who "came up to Paris every week," and that alone gave a hint of the sort of person they had to deal with. . . .

On that Friday, a car stopped outside . . . the green sports car. . . .

Maigret, walking on, reached the Pont-Neuf. An empty taxi passed.

"Rue Caulaincourt."

"What number?"

"I'll tell you when to stop."

He might have waited until morning. In fact, he should have. What he was doing was definitely irregular, but it wasn't the first time. After all, criminals didn't hamper themselves with any qualms about legality!

He didn't feel like going home to bed. He certainly wouldn't be able to sleep. And he had to do something to fill in the time.

"A little farther up on the left . . . There, that white shop . . . Wait for me, will you?"

The dairy. He had to ring three times, though the bell made such a noise that he expected it to wake the whole house. Finally, there was a little click, and the door opened to his touch. Inside, he groped for the light, then tapped on the door of the concierge's lodge.

"The people who keep the dairy, please . . ."

"What do you want? . . . Who are you?"

She finally woke up, opened the door, and thrust out a head covered with curlers.

"I want the dairy people. . . . What? . . . Behind the shop? . . . They have no bell? . . . And Emma, the girl who works for them?"

Ah! Emma slept up on the seventh floor, where her employers rented one of the servants' rooms.

"Thank you madame . . . You needn't worry. I won't disturb anyone else."

After the third floor, he couldn't find any switches, so he had to use matches. On the seventh floor, he found the third door, as he had been told. He knocked gently and put his ear to the door. Through it he heard something like a sigh, then the creaking of bedsprings.

He knocked again.

A sleepy voice: "Who's that?"

He spoke in a loud whisper, for fear of rousing the neighbors.

"Let me in. It's me, the superintendent."

Bare feet on the floorboards. The light went on. More footsteps. Finally, a bolt shot back, and the door opened just wide enough to show the fat girl in her nightgown, her features swollen with sleep, her eyes frightened.

"What do you want?"

The room smelled of bed, woman, a faint whiff of face powder, and soapy water.

"What do you want?"

He shut the door behind him. Emma slipped an old coat on over her nightgown.

"He's been arrested."

"Who has?"

"The murderer . . . The man with the green sports car."

"What?"

She was slow in coming to her senses.

"I tell you he's just been arrested. You've got to come at once to the Quai des Orfèvres to identify him."

"My God! My God!"

"Get dressed quickly. Don't be afraid. I'll look the other way."

He turned his back and heard her fumbling for her underclothes, which he had seen in a heap on a chair by the bed.

"My God! My God!" she repeated.

She was crying, making little sobs. Fifty times she repeated: "My God!" Then: "How is it possible?"

When he turned around, she was still in her pink underwear and was pulling on her stockings. But he had seen plenty of women in his time. As for her, she was too upset to realize she was dressing in front of a man.

"You'll know him, won't you?"

"I'll have to see him. I'll have to . . ."

All at once she threw herself on the bed, sobbing loudly, shaking her head, and protesting.

"I won't! . . . I won't! . . . It's my fault that you've caught him. . . ."

What a chance for a photographer, if one had been there! The massive Maigret in that tiny room, leaning over a fat girl in pink underwear, tapping her on the shoulder!

"Take it easy, my girl. . . . Finish your dressing. . . . They're waiting. . . ."

She went on shaking her head. She bit the sheet and clutched her pillow as though she meant to cling to the bed at all costs.

"Steady now, steady! You've made trouble enough as it is. . . . If I hadn't put in a good word for you, you'd be in prison yourself by now."

That magic word had an instantaneous effect. She looked up.

"In prison?"

"Yes. And for a long time, too. Don't you realize that by refusing to recognize his photograph you've made yourself an accessory?"

She bit her underlip until it bled. An obstinate look came over her face.

"Why?"

"Because . . . because I liked him."

"Well, you've wasted a lot of our time, and he might have slipped through our fingers. . . . We might even have arrested an innocent man. . . . Get dressed. Otherwise I'll be forced to call the policeman who's downstairs."

They were a strange couple creeping down the stairs in the dark. The taxi was waiting.

"Get in."

On the way, Emma's voice returned.

"Why did he kill her? . . . She was his mistress, wasn't she? . . . Other men used to go there. I suppose he was jealous. . . ."

"Maybe."

"I'm sure that was it. He loved her."

He led her up the stairs of the PJ and down the long corridor, where only one lamp was kept on during the night. Janvier, hearing steps, peered out of one of the rooms and was astonished to see his chief with the dairymaid.

"What are they doing?" asked the superintendent.

"The girl is asleep. The other one is waiting."

Maigret took Emma into his office and shut the door.

"Where is he?"

"They're getting him now. He won't be long. Sit down." Poor child – so pink and fresh usually, now pale as a ghost.

"Here are the photographs we showed you. . . ."

He picked them up, as though casually, and handed them to her, one by one, reading the names as he did so.

"Justin-le-Tatoué . . . Bébert from Montpellier . . . La Caille . . ."

She gazed at them petrified, waiting for the one she dreaded. Everything, for Maigret, depended on this moment. He didn't dare look at her face, for fear of warning her. It was her hands he looked at, fat hands with broken nails. One lay on the desk, while the other hung in midair, over the photographs.

"Little Louis from Belleville . . . Justin . . ."

He held his breath for a moment, then suddenly relaxed. It was all over. The finger muscles of both her hands had contracted spasmodically.

"That's him, isn't it? . . . Justin. Justin from Toulon . . ."

She shivered. The expression on her face changed, and she looked up at him blankly.

"Didn't you know?"

The next moment she realized what she'd done. She half rose from the chair. For a second it looked as if she was going to throw herself on the superintendent.

"It isn't true! You haven't arrested him. . . . It was merely a trick to get me to give him away! . . . And I've . . . I've done it! . . . I . . ."

"Gently! Gently! . . . And let me tell you that your precious Justin is a vicious fellow . . ."

"It was I . . . I . . ."

"Come on! You're tired. And you have to get up early. . . . We'll take you home."

He rang.

"Here, Janvier! Take this girl home. . . . Be kind to her, because she's upset. In fact, if you've got a drop of something to make her feel better . . ."

Still, she was not really to be pitied. She'd had a lucky escape. If Justin had taken an interest in her, it might have been a very different story!

10

"Hello! . . . Police Judiciaire? . . . Madame Maigret. Has my husband gone away somewhere?"

"No, my dear, he's here all right!"

"Oh, it's you! Aren't you coming home?"

"Perhaps . . . It all depends. . . ."

Madame Maigret had waked up at four o'clock and had been concerned at finding herself alone in bed.

"No, I'm not going away. . . . Not far, anyway . . . Go back to bed and don't worry."

Alone in his office, he made a whole series of telephone calls, which made him feel rather like the conductor of an orchestra.

"No, Superintendent, Mascouvin can't be questioned yet. Not for another three or four days."

The Criminal Police in Toulon. Then the Criminal Police in Nice.

"Justin, yes . . . We'll do our best. . . . I understand. Glad to help."

Obviously Justin wasn't liked down there!

Through the nearest police station to Rue Notre-Dame-de-Lorette he got hold of Torrence, who was covering Monsieur Blaise, and told him to bring the latter to the PJ later that morning.

Maigret put on his hat, but before leaving he couldn't resist the pleasure of looking through the keyhole at Madame

Le Cloaguen, who still sat rigidly upright in her chair. He couldn't see Lucas, but could hear him snoring.

Day was breaking. The air was full of humidity, and the sidewalks were strewn with wet leaves, but it was no longer raining.

"Taxi! . . . Have you got plenty of gasoline? We have a long trip to make."

At eight o'clock Antoinette Le Cloaguen, her face haggard, but still preserving her dignity, broke the long silence.

"How much longer does your superintendent intend to keep us here?"

Lucas had gone over to the sink and was washing his hands and face.

"Would you rather go straight to prison?"

Her daughter's hair was tousled, like mesh falling over her face. Janvier had managed to get a couple of hours' sleep on a couch in the waiting room. The PJ began to come to life.

At nine, the various superintendents gathered in the room of the "big chief" for the daily staff meeting. Only Maigret was missing.

"Which of you knows about this?"

He read out a message that had been phoned in by the Criminal Police in Nice to the effect that Justin de Toulon had been arrested at seven o'clock that morning as he was leaving the Casino de la Jetée. The man had protested vigorously.

"That must be for Maigret."

"He's not in his office?"

The director went into the next room to inquire, and was astonished to find the two women, who looked like they'd been there all night. He greeted them mechanically.

Seeing the older one coming toward him, he beat a hasty retreat.

"Who was that?" she asked as the door closed.

"The big chief," Lucas answered.

"Really? . . . You mean the director? . . . Tell him I want to see him."

"Impossible! The staff meeting's on."

A Paris taxi splashed through the mud of a little road between Morsang and Fontainebleu, or, more exactly, between the Morsang and the Citanguette locks. It had already stopped at two riverside inns.

"Tell me, have you, by any chance . . ."

He held out the photographs, one in particular. . . . A shake of the head . . . Maigret downed a small glass.

They had been held up at one place by a tree that had been blown down and was lying right across the road. Fortunately, some road workers had turned up with a crane and soon hauled it clear.

"Tell me, have you . . ."

People looked with amazement at this big, unshaven man who smoked pipe after pipe but seemed tireless.

Finally a man said: "Yes, of course . . . Almost every Sunday . . . Fellow with a green sports car."

For the third time, the examining magistrate telephoned Maigret's office.

"No, Monsieur Magistrate, he's not here yet, but he just called to say he'd be back in a quarter of an hour. . . . Yes . . . Monsieur Blaise? . . . He's in another room, with Torrence. . . . Says he's going to take it up with the minister . . . Yes . . . Madame Le Cloaguen? . . . Just the same . . .

Yes, I had coffee and croissants brought in for them. The mother drank her coffee but didn't eat anything. . . ."

Everyone was waiting for Maigret. The director was uncomfortable about the whole thing, because he was receiving protests from all sides. Mademoiselle Berthe, whom Maigret had summoned by express letter, was sitting demurely in the waiting room in her little red hat.

They would have been surprised, all of them, including old Picard, waiting in the Dépôt, had they seen the superintendent at that moment.

He was sprawled across the back seat of the taxi, and at first sight you might have thought him drunk. His eyes were almost closed. No, not quite. Open just enough for him to be vaguely conscious of the green countryside flitting past the window.

Still smoking his eternal pipe, he was lost in a reverie, a reverie that consisted of a strange game in which human beings were pawns. The game was to put each pawn in its proper place.

It was all so simple! . . . And yet so complicated! . . . If only that silly fool hadn't started them off on the wrong foot. Yes, he had a grudge against Mascouvin, who, with his head in bandages, was still lying in a bed at the Hôtel-Dieu. If it hadn't been for him . . .

At the same time Maigret couldn't help feeling indulgent toward him. After all, it was entirely for the sake of that charming little sister of his . . .

To understand the case, it was necessary to understand Mascouvin, the man who was dishonest and conscientious at the same time. He had failed and was tormented by remorse. . . .

It boiled down to a matter of accounting: credits and debits. On the one hand, the salary of a clerk at Proud and Drouin; on the other, the cost of Mademoiselle Berthe's education and furnishing her little apartment, to say nothing of what he needed to keep himself going.

Obviously, his salary was not sufficient.

Yet Monsieur Drouin had said there was no money for the clerk to steal.

At every bump in the road, Maigret's head wobbled and his pipe nearly fell out of his mouth. However, he never lost the thread of the dissertation he was to give presently in his office at the Quai des Orfèvres, by which time all the pawns had to be in their proper places. . . .

"Yes, Magistrate, that was the start of everything. . . . Mascouvin was tempted. . . . By whom? By one of the firm's clients, a man who rarely bought anything but was interested in everything they had to offer. . . . Monsieur Blaise, in fact, the most cunning and pitiless of blackmailers . . .

"A beautifully organized business! He has accomplices, but is never seen with them. None of them ever sets foot in his apartment on Rue Notre-Dame-de-Lorette, where he passes for a model citizen, a respectable man of private means.

"At Morsang, at the Pretty Pigeon, he's an enthusiastic fisherman. He fishes in the tall reeds and rushes of the bank, where he's hidden from view."

Only that morning, Maigret had forced the admission out of Isidore.

"Yes, I've always done his fishing for him. He goes in for another sport! Meets a woman up there. A married woman, I suppose, but I don't know who she is. I've never seen her. . . . Nobody suspects what he's really after. . . ."

A married woman? Nothing of the kind. Who, then, came to meet him between the Morsang and Citanguette locks?

Who would the careful Monsieur Blaise need for his business? Someone to collect money and get tough with those who didn't want to pay.

That was Justin's role. Justin with the green sports car.

What other people did he need? People to supply him with information that others would pay to have kept quiet.

That's where Mascouvin came in. He and others. He worked in a real estate office, where, among other things, they dealt with new housing. Plenty of shady business there! Concessions to be acquired, local regulations to be by-passed, municipal officials' palms to be greased!

Monsieur Drouin had been quite right. Mascouvin had no access to any of the firm's money. He could read the firm's letters, however, and copy compromising paragraphs. Much safer. More lucrative too! Lucrative enough to buy the pretty Mademoiselle Berthe all she needed.

He had been tempted. And once he was entangled in Monsieur Blaise's web there was no getting free again. He was caught – an honest man who has slipped and is condemned to be dishonest for the rest of his life.

It was torture to him. He was tortured too by the indifference of the countess, with whom he'd fallen in love.

He was anxious, complicated. As Drouin had said, he was a man who was always conscientious, and who went wrong.

"Why? . . . I'll tell you, Magistrate. . . ."

Maigret tapped on the glass partition. They were at one of the gates in Paris. At the Quai des Orfèvres, everyone was waiting for him.

"Stop here, driver. . . . I'm thirsty."

It was true. Though that wasn't why he was stopping. The thing was he hadn't yet finished the game. He hadn't yet got his pawns into position.

"What about Mademoiselle Jeanne?" the examining magistrate would ask.

"Another of Blaise's informers . . . A fortuneteller! . . .

What better profession for ferreting out people's secrets? . . . Regularly every Friday Justin came to collect the week's confidences, which he would then hand over to Blaise, the fisherman, under cover of the rushes on the riverbank.

"How did she get involved in this business? Impossible to say. All we know about her is that her mother wasn't much good, that her father became a tramp, and that she herself had had a pretty desperate struggle to keep her head above water. . . . Perhaps, like our friend Emma, she had fallen for the handsome Justin. . . .

"Then one day Justin stumbled on the Le Cloaguen hoax. He saw the old man coming away from his daughter's house and no doubt followed him home to Boulevard des Batignolles.

"A perfect little gold mine! A woman with an ill-gotten income of two hundred thousand francs a year! She was the ideal victim. Henceforth she would have to share it. And Blaise would get the lion's share!"

Maigret was sitting near the counter of the little bar, and the driver began to wonder whether he hadn't fallen asleep. The game was still going on, however.

"I assure you, Magistrate, that that's what happened. Mademoiselle Jeanne learned that Justin was going to deal with Madame Le Cloaguen, and her father was bound to take the recoil. She pleaded. Perhaps she threatened to give the whole thing away, to denounce them all.

"So, it was decided to kill the fortuneteller!

"It was much too good a deal to be abandoned for sentimental reasons. Even if, for them, she was a goose that laid golden eggs. . . . And they'd decided to ask Madame Le Cloaguen for a whole year's annuity. . . . It was decided on. They'd kill Mademoiselle Jeanne at five o'clock on Friday."

At the Quai des Orfèvres they were getting more and more impatient. So was the taxi driver, who had been at work all night and was longing to get home to bed.

"Another calva, landlord."

It was decided. The fortuneteller was to be killed. Only, why was Mascouvin told about it? . . . Perhaps he had been kicking too. Anyhow, it would be a good lesson to him. Raise the standard of discipline in the gang . . .

What could the wretched Mascouvin do? Could he go to the police and say: "I belong to a gang of blackmailers, and one of us is going to be killed at five o'clock tomorrow. She's a fortuneteller, but I don't know her name or where she lives. . . ."

Hardly. But the conscientious crook had to do something. He turned it over and over in his mind as he sat in the Café des Sports. . . . An anonymous letter to the police? . . . They'd take no notice. He must go himself.

He had a bright idea. The blotting-paper trick . . . Disguising his handwriting, he wrote a note, blotted it. He'd take the blotter to the police.

Really quite clever . . . When he finished the note, he caught sight of the calendar and signed it *Picpus.*

He'd only have to keep out of Justin's reach for a while. For that, he invented the story of the thousand francs he'd stolen from Proud and Drouin. In prison he'd be safe.

A complicated creature, Mascouvin. Too complicated . . . But then, when you're conscientious! . . . And a crook as well! . . .

When he failed to stop the murder, his one thought was to do away with himself. . . .

"Hey! Wake up!"

The taxi driver shook Maigret's shoulder. The superintendent really had gone to sleep this time. He opened his eyes.

"Where shall I take you?"

"Quai des Orfèvres."

"Eh?"

"Police Judiciaire."

So profoundly had he slept that it took him the whole way to pull himself together. He needed all his faculties. True, the game was over, but the real job lay before him, that of explaining it to the examining magistrate.

One good thing anyhow had come out of Monsieur Blaise's infamous activities. They had stopped Madame Le Cloaguen. If it hadn't been for them, she'd have gone on forever hoarding the annuities and browbeating her tame tramp.

What a nasty woman!

The PJ . . . Maigret walked gloomily up the stairs.

"They're all waiting for you, Superintendent."

"I know . . . I know . . ."

It was noon. Not only was everyone waiting for him, but the faces that were turned on him were full of resentment, especially the face of the examining magistrate, who felt he'd been treated with scant respect.

The explanation lasted until three o'clock.

"But what can you prove?" sneered Monsieur Blaise at the end.

"Everything . . . Justin's come clean."

It was true. A call from Nice earlier had reported that Justin had been lulled into thinking he might save his neck if he talked, and he had given away his boss and all the others.

"Aren't you coming home?" asked Madame Maigret over the telephone.

"In – let's see now – in about an hour . . . What are you having for dinner?"

One last little chore to do. As the examining magistrate

had pointed out, no action could be taken against Madame Le Cloaguen unless the person she had defrauded agreed to prosecute.

The Argentine gentleman who had provided the annuity was dead.

His daughter, whom Octave Le Cloaguen had saved, had, like many another South American heiress, married a foreign prince. They lived in Paris.

A liveried manservant ushered Maigret into the sumptuous living room of a private house near the Etoile. He waited a whole hour. Poor Madame Maigret! Finally the door opened.

"I'm so sorry, Superintendent. . . . These stupid servants! They forgot to tell me you were here. . . . What can I do for you?"

The girl who had nearly died of yellow fever was now a woman of fifty. She still dressed like a debutante, however, and was certainly a much valued customer of somebody's beauty parlor. She was accompanied by a young man who looked like her equerry.

"I suppose you know, madame, that many years ago your father settled an annuity of two hundred thousand francs on a certain Dr. Le Cloaguen . . ."

"Oh, yes, I know. When I had yellow fever . . . Can you imagine me with yellow fever, José?"

"The thing is, Dr. Le Cloaguen died and . . ."

"Poor man! He can't have been old."

"He was . . ."

No, it was better not to discuss people's ages in this house!

"As a matter of fact, he died ten years ago, and his wife, in order not to lose the income, got another man to impersonate him – a tramp she picked up in the streets of Cannes who looked like him."

"How amusing! . . . José, are you listening? . . . I haven't heard anything so funny for ages. . . . Do you mean to say she took him into her house as her husband? . . . Tell me, Superintendent, do you think they . . . ?"

"The point is, madame, that you've been defrauded out of a very considerable sum of money, and I've come to ask you whether you wish to prosecute."

"Prosecute? . . . Why should I?"

"Fraud's a serious matter, madame."

"Poor woman! . . . Why didn't she write to me? I'd have arranged it all at once. To tell the truth, I'd forgotten all about it. It's my lawyer who sees to matters of that sort. . . . But no, Superintendent . . . Tell me . . . I'd like to meet the woman who . . . It's too funny! A new husband who's the same . . . ! Isn't that interesting, José? Do you think she'd come and have tea with me, Superintendent?"

"Maigret! . . . Here you are at last! . . . I was wondering whether you'd ever come. . . . I've got some *fricandeau* waiting for you."

But as he crossed the hall the superintendent began taking off his jacket and loosening his tie.

"Sleep," he murmured.

"What? . . . Do you mean to say you're not going to eat anything? . . . You?"

He didn't answer, but dived straight into the bedroom. As he undressed, he muttered to himself.

"What fools . . . What fools people are! . . ."

But as he finally laid his head on the pillow, his face relaxed into a dreamy smile.

If they weren't such fools, there'd be no need of policemen. . . .